SERGEANT

KEITH J. WALKER

Cover Photo: Korean War Memorial,
Washington DC, Kali Mccauley
ISBN 978-0-9882725-1-4

DEDICATED TO THE MEN OF THE

1st Recon Squadron
9th Calvary Regiment
1st Calvary Division

CONTENTS

PREFACE / 1990

My kid is writing this story. I'm an old fart now, born in 1918 and still sucking air but not for much longer. I was a sergeant in the Army of the United States for forty years. I killed a lot of people, mostly other soldiers just trying to do their job. I never got married, but I have five kids and a bunch of grand kids. None of my women would marry me except one and she was killed before we could get hitched. I have a lot of friends scattered around the world, but my two very best friends were a hermaphrodite and a Bengal Tiger. This story is as much about them as it is about me.

Lewis Sergeant
Sergeant Major
United States Army

SERGEANT

Dad told me to leave out the 'racy' parts of his life but I'm not going to do that. He is over seventy now and not a spry seventy either. His body is shot to hell and he's getting grouchy and why not? He was a sergeant all his army life and sergeants lead from the front, not the rear. Pop was never married, but some of the things he did between wars are the 'racy parts' that I plan to include in his story. His extended family and most of his living friends recorded a lot of the stuff I used although some of it should be X rated.

He gets confused when he's around a crowd of people, especially Asians. He sometimes speaks Vietnamese to Koreans and vice versa, and calls Germans Huns one minute and Krauts the next. Some of his friends he plans to visit have been dead for years, and some of his words and idiomatic expressions can only be found in old American ballads, or in the histories of other countries. Like me, all of us kids are bastards. Most of our mothers are married and some are single, but we all have something in common—green eyes.

THE SERGEANTS / 1918 - 1938

1

Bill and Nancy Sergeant had three sons, and the youngest they named Lewis after the great explorer Meriwether Lewis. He was a hell raiser from the start and when he learned to crawl he found a framing hammer and pounded nails into everything, the floors, the walls and even his dad's shoes. The first thing he did when he stood up was to climb a ladder to the roof and pound nails in the shingles. Bill was a logger and tough as wang leather, and disciplined his sons with his leather stoup. When Lewis started walking he got his share. The boys never cried as crying was good for a few more whacks. He didn't start talking until he was three; he just made sounds, like a kettle on the boil or someone chopping wood. Drove his Ma crazy; she was always running around looking for fallen dishes, slamming doors and the like. He was a born mimic but his family did not appreciate his talent or understand his love of animals. He would often sit for hours watching and listening to sometimes inaudible sounds, then he would communicate. A grunt or snort or just a gesture. The boy could literally charm the birds out of the trees.

Lewis started reading at four, and read everything in the house including the Bible. The he grew like a weed and started school when he was five. On the first day of school his mother fell to her knees and thanked the Lord.

It was a two-room school house; and first to fourth grades were in one room and fifth to eighth were in the other. He was the tallest boy in the first grade and the best student, so he was moved to the fifth grade in the other room.

The high school was in the little logging town of Cottage Grove, Oregon and Lewis was the youngest freshman in the class. High school was a trial of terror for the freshmen. They had to wear beanies to show their lowly status. They were pushed and kicked; their faces were ground into the mud, and woe to the boy that cried. He was labeled a crybaby, and shunned by the whole school. The first day at recess Lewis had a beanie crammed on his head and was pushed into a circle of yelling upper classmen. Lewis picked out the leader of the pack, walked over and kicked him in the balls. After years of fighting with two older brothers, a high school bully was just a nuisance A day later he found the school library. It was like an Arab finding Mecca. Books, books and more books, history, physics, geography…the whole room was crammed with books. The teachers had to drag him into class.

At fourteen, Lewis was hit by the blessing, or curse, of

puberty. In a blaze of hormonal chaos he discovered that little girls changed into big girls with tits. He was not a handsome boy. Not with a nose like an ax blade, crooked teeth and hair like a palm tree. But he had remarkable green eyes, was almost six feet tall, and was comfortable with women. To hell with books, he was going to play football; it attracted girls. The first day of spring practice he breezed through the workouts. He was big, weighed 165 pounds, not very fast runner but quick as a cat, and he remembered everything. The second week of training the coach had the second string scrimmage against the Varsity. In the 1930's the players wore leather helmets, no padding and played both offense and defense. The first play Lewis flattened the left guard and hit the runner hard enough to put him out for the season. The coach stopped the scrimmage and Lewis and two other freshmen started for the Varsity.

Their first home game was against the hated Eugene Bobcats and Cottage Grove won with ease. The fans, (everyone in town), decided the team needed a real gym, so they all chipped in and built a nice building with lockers, a weight room and a large shower room. In the middle of the depression, "chipping in" was a monumental task. The mills gave all the lumber, the merchants the fixtures, the men did the labor and the women fed the crew. In that new shower room the boys saw, with a few quick glances, that Mister Lewis Sergeants nose was not the only big thing he had.

In the thirties, women were divided into two classes, good girls and bad girls. Good girls kept their panties on,

3

their brassieres locked and their legs crossed. Bad girls had their tits felt up or screwed a boyfriend who said he loved her and then bragged of his 'conquest.' Good could slide into bad but bad could never slide back, and many a girls' reputation was destroyed by a liar. It was especially true in high school. Mary Ann Brown was one of the bad girls, but she was different. She enjoyed sex and did not give a damn what others thought. Mary was picky about her sexual partners, and if one of them bragged about his 'conquest', he was cut off. If one of her few friends mentioned the matter, she would laugh and say, "You mean old pencil dick?" and her erstwhile partner would be the subject of many a giggle.

Lewis liked her; she was smart, pretty and easy to talk to. Lewis was a senior by then, a football hero, and had the second highest grades in school, so Mary was surprised when he sat by her in the lunch room. The next day they sat together in the library studying for a history exam. She liked him and as their friendship grew she began to wonder why he was so interested in the school slut. Two months before graduation he asked her out to dinner. She agreed, and the next day she picked him up in her father's Ford, and they drove to a small restaurant in Eugene. Mary thought that the meal was not conducive to foreplay. Men kept stopping to ask if he was going to play college football at Eugene. On the way home Lewis was ranting about the 'hero' business.

"You know Mary, none of those jokers even looked at you. It's the same way in football, one shining knight and ten spear carriers."

"Poor baby, she snorted, "You couldn't be a knight in shining armor anyway."

"Why's that?"

"Couldn't get a helmet visor over that big beak of yours." He laughed at that shot and poked her in the ribs where the tickle spot lurked.

"Stop it Lewis," she yelled as the Ford drifted towards the ditch. They rode in silence for a minute…then.

"Lewis, may I ask you a personal question?"

"Shoot."

"Why haven't you tried to get into my pants? God knows you've had plenty of opportunities."

"I thought you knew Mary."

"Knew what…cut the crap Lewis, knew what?" Lewis looked out the window for a moment, then turned with a sad look on his face.

"I'm queer," he said quietly and Mary almost drove off the road.

"Bullshit Lewis, I know that you don't fool around at home but at other schools some of those cheerleaders are walking around bowlegged." Lewis was quiet for a moment thinking. *An honest question deserves an honest answer.*

"Mary you are a very good looking woman, not a girl, but a woman. You are also very intelligent, have a great sense of humor, and are fun to be with. But every guy in school sees you as a target, not a person, just tits and ass."

"I know all about the T & A stuff but you haven't answered my question."

"You're no target to me. First move is up to you."

Mary responded by slamming on the brakes, and bouncing the car up an old logging track. She stopped behind a bush, reached over and rubbed his crotch. "How's that for a first move," she said peeling off her clothes. While Lewis was getting his shoes and shirt off, Mary was digging in her purse for her box of rubbers. They tried to put one on but it broke. When the second one split they both started giggling and Lewis started to droop.

"God Mary, how old are these things?" Mary said, "what the hell," and slid down to his lap.

"Pull out when I say to", she groaned.

"How the hell can I pull out with you on my lap?"

They found a mossy bed and made love until dawn. Driving home Mary reached over and held his hand.

"Lewis," I've been with a lot of boys but this the first time I ever made love." Later she found out that Lewis hadn't been quick enough.

Mary and Lewis graduated with honors. Mary had the highest grades in the school's history and Lewis finished second in the class of 1936. A month after graduation Mary disappeared. Her parents would not talk to him, but he found her…years later.

Lewis decided that he was not going to college and neither friends nor family could change his mind. He wanted to work in the woods with his father and brothers. His oldest brother was a high climber, the man that topped the spar trees that would give lift, so the logs would clear

6

the stumps as they were pulled to the landing. They were loaded on flatcars and pulled by small "lokies" on narrow gauge tracks and sent to the mill. His younger brother was a faller and worked with his dad.

Working down among the huge logs was brutal. The green choker men had to catch one of the flying chokers dancing from a forty foot cable. The green men always started on the chokers. Five men waited for four chokers. The four men that caught one did a day's work; the fifth man went home, if he was able. The men that were killed were laid by the tracks and sent back with the last load of logs.

Like most local boys starting in the woods, Lewis worked with his father and brothers. They were his guardians and mentors, teaching him the skills and hazards of logging. In the days of steam logging during the depression, men had to get logs to the mill fast and cheap, as the mills needed cheap logs to produce cheap lumber to survive. But fast and cheap killed many skilled loggers trying to get in one more log before quitting time. In a year, Lewis learned enough to stay alive, and in his second year he was considered a skilled logger.

In the evenings the Sergeant family would listen to Walter Winchell broadcast the evening news on the radio. Like most Americans, they remembered the carnage of the American Civil War, and The Great War in Europe. Bill Sergeant had lost two brothers in France and did not want any part of European problems. He hated war, Germans, politicians and in that order.

"The war killed a generation of young men all because of Royalty," he would say, "and now we've got the Nazi and the Commie waiting to kill more young men." As usual Lewis had a different opinion on Nazi Germany and Hitler. He started working on his German and French after he read Hitler's book mien Kampf. *War is coming,* he thought, *it's going to be a great adventure, and I'm going to be part of it.*

MARY ANN BROWN

2

Mary's father had immigrated from Germany as a young man and had worked as a clerk in a large department store in Portland. He worked hard at his job and his English and in a few years he was promoted to accounting where he, like Saul on the road to Damascus, had an epiphany. Not a wage slave but a business man! He changed his name to Emeritus Brown and married a small, hardly visible, Dutch girl and moved to Cottage Grove. With his accounting skills Mr. Brown was able to work at the towns small bank, and by some small miracle, was able to impregnate Missis Brown. With his savings and a loan from the bank he bought a small store with a tiny apartment in the attic. Emeritus Brown, by that one bold move, stepped up from working class to middle class. Another miracle was the birth of a baby girl christened Mary Ann Brown.

Some time ago a mutant gene was introduced into the long Brown line. The invisible Missis Brown had an older sister who was very visible. Ida Mann blew through Cottage Grove one or twice a year on her way to some meeting or protest and once proudly to jail. She was a Free Thinker, dabbled in the 'Arts', believed in Free Love and was sterile. The gene skipped a generation and was passed on to Mary Ann Brown.

"Pop I'm pregnant," she announced at supper as Emeritus was finishing his desert.

"That's bad for business" he blurted out. "Who's the father? The Sergeant boy. That's not too bad, the Sergeants pay their bills on time. He'll marry you and we'll have a quick wedding and no one will be the wiser." He was mentally totaling up the cost of a proper wedding when Mary gently interrupted.

"Daddy there is not going to be any wedding. Lewis doesn't know I'm pregnant and I'm not about to tell him."

"Why not? The Sergeant boys are good workers and Ben is going to be promoted to woods boss. Your scholarship at …" he trailed off. Pregnant women did not get scholarships, period.

"Lewis would marry me in a second. Then what? Poor Lewis, she mimicked. "He knocked up that Brown girl and had to marry her. "I will not put up with that kind of garbage about me or about Lewis."

"What will you do?"

"I'm going to Idaho and stay with Aunt Ida, and you and mom are not going to tell Lewis where I am or that I'm pregnant."

"Mary, Ida is a bomb throwing anarchist and a suffragette. She has Orofino stirred up enough to get her lynched."

"My kind of people," she grinned.

"Why not tell Lewis. It's his child and he should know he's going to be a father."

"Because Lewis would don his shining armor and hunt me down. He has his own dreams and marriage would end them. I don't want that, Daddy. I'm going to be a mother, and I'll be a good one."

WORLD WAR II / 1939 - 1945

3

In 1939, Lewis, along with dozens of other Americans, sailed on the HMS *Athenia* from Canada to England. The trip was uneventful, but on the return voyage, the ship was torpedoed by a German U boat and sunk. This was the beginning of the great battle of the Atlantic which claimed the lives of thousands of merchant seamen. In London, Lewis signed up with the British Army and was sent to an infantry unit that was to be part of the British Expeditionary Force, or BEF. In the hastily built camps, the recruits were trained using wooden rifles. The Australians in the group claimed that the rifles only fired termites. Lewis was promoted to corporal and later, in France, due to luck, skill and attrition, he would be promoted to sergeant.

In 1940, advance units of the BEF embarked to France and were posted along the Maginot Line. This line of concrete fortifications between France and Germany was considered impregnable and was given only a token force of the BEF, while a much larger group of several divisions reinforced the French on the Belgian border. This period became known as the 'phony war', a lull in the slaughter of World War II. Lewis had studied German and French in the States and had become fluent in German and was rapidly improving his French. Following the adage of 'know your enemy', he had studied the writings of the great military planners, such as Von Clausewitz and Schlieffen. He thought that these brilliant men would ignore the Maginot line and simply go around it. However he had faith in the French army, which outnumbered the Germans and was reinforced by the BEF. He spent his spare time scouting the terrain and mapping routs for a retreat just in case of a German breakthrough. His scouting was considered defeatism by his superiors and he was ordered to stay in the ranks.

The German Blitzkrieg went through the Maginot line as if it did not exist, paratroops going over it and tanks and infantry around it. Lewis's unit was pulled from guarding the rear to reconing the terrain ahead of the retreating division. It was rifles and feet against the German Panzers, and the Maginot line became a concrete prison for thousands of French soldiers. The advance units commandeered anything with wheels or hooves to move the troops, and thousands of tons of fuel, equipment and food were left to the advancing Germans. The order went out, 'to hell with the equipment, save the men.'

At Dunkirk, one division of the BEF and two French divisions were dug in a defensive line to protect the lines of troops waiting on the beach. Hundreds of British vessels, from destroyers to sailboats, were taking on the men that had waded up to their necks to reach them. The ships were under constant bombardment from the Luftwaffe, strafing and bombing both ships and men, killing hundreds, even with the RAF desperately trying to protect them. Lewis's unit was part of the defense. They had abandoned their rifles for machineguns and had ramped them up on sandbags to shoot down aircraft. His best gunner led off with tracers, and the others followed his lead, letting the plane fly into a cone of fire.

With the lines of embarking men getting shorter, Lewis decided that it was time to leave or be taken prisoner. His commander spoke to the French commander, who gave his men permission to leave if they desired. Most of the French accepted, but a few chose to stay defending their homeland. That night Lewis and his men pulled out of the line and waded out to a cluster of small boats carrying their weapons. A small boy waved at Lewis and some of his men, and a squeaky voice told them to board. The boat was the *Tamzine*, the smallest boat with the youngest crew to cross the channel. Winston Churchill called the evacuation the 'Miracle of Dunkirk' which allowed over 400,000 Allied soldiers to fight another day.

In England the great air battle between the Royal Air Force and Goring's Luftwaffe had begun. The arrivals from Dunkirk were shuttled to camps on the large country estates owned by England's wealthiest families. After a few days rest, Lewis was told to report back to London for a debriefing by British intelligence. From London he was sent to Dover and into the great labyrinth of tunnels and rooms that were cut into the white chalk cliffs. Lewis was led into a large room filled with officers. He saw a French captain he knew and liked from Dunkirk, and his old company commander who he respected. He also noticed that he was the only sergeant in the room, and settled down for a long wait. He was surprised to hear his name called. The questions were short and Lewis's answers were blunt. The Officer in Charge summed up the interview.

"In short Sergeant you believe that the defeat of Allied forces was caused by the following: Overconfidence in the Maginot Line; No secondary line of defense prepared; Inferior anti-tank weapons; Poor intelligence; Inadequate transportation for troop movement; and ignorance of available German tactical plans. Does that sum it up?" Lewis nodded and stood up to leave. "Your unit shot down several German fighters at Dunkirk. How did you manage that?" Lewis told him and for the first time the officer smiled. "A good duck hunter eh, I'll have to remember that one."

The Army was not finished with Sergeant Lewis. He was recalled to London and left cooling his heels in a bleak wartime office with several British and French officers. Lewis was summoned to a large conference room and into the presence of a British Major General, several staff officers and two civilians. The General opened with the remark that, "The Sergeant here is a bit of a problem for the Army", he continued. "He has been recommended for the Military Cross, but the decoration has never been given to a foreign soldier." He looked at Lewis and said, "Thank you Sergeant, you are dismissed." When Lewis had left the officers waiting outside were called in including his Company Commander and the French Commander at Dunkirk. They both told the General that if it had not been for Lewis's recon platoon many of them would be dead or prisoners of war. The General remarked that the honor would please our American cousins. Lewis's CO snapped out that the sergeant earned the decoration.

"Right now the British people need hero's from any country."

The award ceremony was held with all the pomp and ceremony available to the British armed forces in wartime. Medals were presented by King George V for the British and by General de Gaulle for the French. The Victoria Cross was presented to the widows and mothers of the men killed in France. Not one living member received England's highest award. The reception was held in Buckingham Palace with the cream of London Society attending along with men and women in uniforms of all branches of the armed forces. Many of the uniforms were from the Commonwealth countries of Great Britain's vast empire. The King made a brief appearance and retired. The atmosphere of the reception changed with the departure of the King. The defeat of the BEF, the air battle over Britain, and the threat of invasion gave the partygoers a live-for-the-moment attitude, and soon young couples were pairing off and seeking hidden spots in the gardens.

Lewis was ready to leave when he looked up and into the eyes of a woman. She was a young French widow who had been at the medal ceremony. He walked over to ask her to dance, but instead of the dance floor they took the stairs to one of the hundred bedrooms in the palace. Her name was Dominique and was the widow of a soldier killed in the German Blitzkrieg through Belgium. "I need a man" she said and started removing her clothes.

Dominique was a woman of high spirits with a love of life. She was a lusty wench and took few precautions during sex. She did not like doing it in a garden or on the beach as she crudely put it, she did not like 'sand in her crack or thorns in her ass'. Lewis asked her several times to marry him, but she always refused. "Neither you nor I will survive this war," she said, then told him that she was learning how to be a radio operator, and was going back to France to join the resistance. Lewis returned to his unit and a month later when he came back she was gone. A year later he learned from another Frenchwoman that she had been captured by the Gestapo, tortured and hung with piano wire to die in a cellar.

Lewis was depressed. Dominique had left him feeling desolate and alone. He took up boxing but he found little pleasure in it. He entered the division shooting contest easily winning as he never missed at any distance.

A little man, that had been watching the contest, came

over and introduced himself. His name was Weaver, and he was one of the best gunsmiths in the world. He told Lewis that his two handed stance should be used instead of that one handed business. Weaver asked how come he never missed.

"It's the wires," Lewis replied. "I never use a sight; the bullet follows the wires to the target."

"Can you see these wires," Weaver asked? "

"Of course" Lewis laughed, "how else could I hit the target?" They started talking about weapons of war. Lewis asked him if he could make a .50 caliber sniper rifle, scope mounted and completely silent. Weaver thought for a moment, and then told him that a .50 caliber rifle would never be completely silent, but would make a noise more like a cough.

"This weapon would kick like a mule and would need to be mounted on a tripod."

"How fast can you build it?"

"I'll have it ready in two weeks," said the little man, "and if you kill at least ten of those Nazi bastards I won't charge you a thing."

The weapon was ready for testing in two weeks. Instead of paper targets, they used mannequins with German helmets and uniforms. The word had gotten out to the shooting community and several dozen men, most in uniform, showed at the range. Two men with spotting scopes volunteered to call the mark corrections. The first target was at 1,000 yards. Aiming at the nose, Lewis fired. "Eleven o'clock, two inches." Lewis tweaked the scope slightly and fired. "Dead center," called the spotters. The second target was at 1,500 yards away and was barely visible to the naked eye. Lewis fired, and the spotters said, "dead center." The last target, at 3000 yards was only a pinhead on the spotting scopes and invisible to the men watching. Lewis spotted a slight ripple in the grass, made a slight adjustment for windage, and fired. The spotters climbed into a jeep and drove out to inspect the target. They returned and held up a German helmet with a hole in the center. The onlookers were silent, each man thinking about the terror that this weapon could cause. In the Great War, a sniper could pick off a careless man at 1,000 yards. This weapon could kill at a distance slightly less than two miles, making battlefield safety an illusion.

"Like the arm of God," one man murmured.

EGYPT

4

Weaver was not shy about promoting his craft, and soon had the attention of the military. The Army wanted to send the weapon to North Africa for field testing under battlefield conditions. The armorers told Lewis that many a weapon that performed well on the range failed in the field. Lewis said that he would go to Africa and take Weaver with him. The little man looked worried at this, as he did not like the sight of blood, especially his own, but the thought of a fat military contract cheered him enough to accept.

They left on a destroyer bound for Egypt to join General Wavell's campaign against the Italians. Their group included Lewis and Weaver, a spotter and an armorer. General Wavell was very interested in the project, and especially the long ugly silencers, and the vented .50 caliber barrels.

"The silencers will hide our location, and the flash guards will only let an enemy directly in front of the weapon see a small spark," Weaver said. "This scope that I designed will gather all the available light, and can be used on clear moonlit nights. The vented barrel is only used with the silencers, as the venting reduces the velocity of the projectile. The bullet is subsonic and very quiet."

The next night, with sand capes and water, they started the five-mile trek to the Italian lines. They headed for a double-topped hill east of the Italian positions. There was an enemy observation post on top of the highest hill, so Lewis placed his team on the lower hill. The Italian observers had a concertina and were singing love songs and enjoying themselves. Lewis, his spotter and two boxes of .50 caliber ammo, were under one cape and Weaver and the Armorer were under the other.

Lewis peered down the scope into the moonless night. At about 1,000 yards there was a large command tent with the sides rolled up to let in the cool night air. In the well-lit tent there was a table strewn with maps and wine bottles. Seven officers were talking and pointing at a map. Lewis waited a minute to determine who was in charge, and when he had marked his man, he gently squeezed the trigger. The weapon coughed and the man disappeared. The singing and drinking on the other hill continued unabated. The remaining officers were transfixed. Their leader was alive one moment and dead the next and without a sound. Lewis picked his next target, a man that seemed to take charge by reaching for a lantern. The weapon coughed again and removed the man's head. The remaining officers ran to their units, screaming orders to their uncomprehending men.

Fear of the unknown can cause panic in the individual and chaos in a group. Fearing an attack, a huge volume of fire was directed at the British lines, causing the Italian observers to run for the safety of their own guns. In the darkness, Lewis waited for the moon. It rose over the horizon, a gibbous moon that vanquished the darkness, a sniper's moon. Seeing no advancing enemy, the Italian fire died down and stopped. Using a powerful pair of ship's glasses, the spotter started to rate the targets. First the officers, then the noncoms and last the gunners. Three officers were standing by a truck, and Lewis quickly killed the first two, but the third man ducked behind the truck. Lewis traversed the weapon and killed two sergeants smoking beside a howitzer. He swung back and killed the third officer who had moved from the protection of the truck. The third officer had not shouted a warning and the rest of the enemy appeared unaware of their danger.

Lewis had learned grouse hunting from his father who was a dead shot. Bill said that the mother hen always went first, looking and clucking, and the young birds followed. His dad would always shoot the birds in the head, starting with the last and working up to the mother. As long as the dead birds behind her were not flopping around she would not look back, and would die last. Lewis looked across the compound for 'young birds', and killed a clerk typing by lantern light. He picked off another dozen noncoms before the alarm was raised and panic stricken men started jumping into trucks and half-tracks and moving away from the

British lines. The next day the Italians retreated to their fortified position at Sidi Barrani.

Lewis, Weaver and the other men returned to England, with the enthusiastic recommendation from General Wavell, that heavy weapons with their long-range capacity would be valuable as infantry support. Seconded by Wavell, Lewis was recruited by Colonel William Darby to train sniping teams for a raid on Dieppe in southern France. Lewis picked his team carefully. The men had to be volunteers in top physical condition, cunning and above all, patient. He picked eight two-man teams, a spotter and a shooter. One team washed out in training because the shooter could not shoot to Lewis's standards.

DIEPPE

5

The raid was on, and the Raiders sailed at night, arriving at Dieppe the following midnight. The squad leader, a Commando Lieutenant, Lewis and his seven teams split from the main force and climbed to the top a ridge and looked down at the German artillery positioned safely on the landward side. They would be able to lob shells over the ridge and be safe from counter-fire from the ships. The ridge top was perfect for snipers with boulders for cover and good lanes of fire. When the Raiders attacked, the teams went to work, starting with the gun captains and their crews. They were spotted by the German artillery observer who called down mortar fire. Team two saw the observer's position and shot him. The snipers moved down the ridge line and, without the observer, the mortar squad lost them. A company of infantry stormed the ridge proceeded by mortar fire, and Lewis was hit in the legs and back by shrapnel. The German troops were veterans, and worked their way up the ridge relentlessly, driving the snipers back to the beach. With their backs to the water, they were saved by the destroyers 4-inch guns that pushed the Germans back to the shelter of the ridge. The teams were picked up by one of the destroyer's boats. No man or weapon of the teams was lost.

Dieppe was a disaster for the Allied forces, especially the Canadians, and thousands of men had been killed or captured. There would be no further action against the German occupiers in France until the Normandy invasion.

Lewis, who was the only wounded member of his sniper unit, was taken to a hospital in London. His back and legs were pitted with shrapnel, with one large vertical wound near his rectum. The doctor told him that if it was one inch closer to the right, he would have a vagina instead of a rectum. An intern spent hours digging metal out of his legs and back.

Colonel Darby came by to visit his wounded men. He had put Lewis and the Lieutenant in for the War Medal for their work on the ridge. Lewis argued that a lot of men, most of them dead, did a lot more than he did. The colonel replied that something had to be salvaged from the disaster, and their teams had kept the German artillery from sinking some of the ships that were needed for the evacuation. He also informed Lewis that he was now part of the American army.

101ST DIVISION

6

While the British and American armies were slogging up the boot of Italy, thousands of men and millions of tons of equipment and supplies were pouring into England from America. The buildup for the invasion of France, Operation Overlord, had begun.

Lewis had wanted to join the fighting in Italy, but the senior command had other ideas on how to use experienced combat veterans; Especially veterans that had fought in France and spoke French and German.

He was assigned to the 101st Airborne Division to train recon units, and give each company a week of intensive training. *Then intensive it will be,* he thought. He was humiliated at being a trainer of snot nose kids who thought they were tough because they wore jump boots. He was a decorated combat veteran and not a babysitter. A few of the noncoms were veterans of the 82nd Airborne that had fought in Italy and they resented being lumped in with the green men of the 101st. They had been sent to the 101st as veteran leaders and were not about to take any crap from a sergeant that had been kicked out France twice by the Germans.

"My name is Lewis Sergeant. I am here to train you how to kill as many Germans as possible before they kill you," he continued. "Since I can out fight, out shoot and out fuck anyone in this sorry outfit, you will obey me." He was about to continue when a voice from the ranks said.

"Cut the crap and get on with it you Limy prick." Lewis the mimic remembered that he still had his English accent from his years in the British army. He smiled
   at the sergeant.

"You are welcome to take my place sergeant. You sound like a southern boy", and added in a soft southern accent, "like a catfish—all mouth and no brains." The sergeant, a big tough Texan from the Piney woods, figured that he had probably made a mistake, but it was too late to back off. Lewis said.

"This is a training session sergeant, here's your bayo-net." and tossed him one from the wooden box at his side. Sergeant McCoy, called 'Mac' pulled the weapon from its sheath. It was a brand new German Mauser K98 bayonet from the Solingen factory and was 13 inches of razor sharp steel.

"The sergeant is holding a fine killing weapon," Lewis went on to explain. "It has hollow ground groves on both

28

sides called 'blood lettors' which keeps the knife from sticking in the guts when it's pulled out. The brass piece between the handle and the blade is called the frog. The softer brass keeps another steel blade from sliding off and into your guts.

"If sergeant—Lewis raised a quizzical eyebrow" "Mac" the sergeant said, "Mac survives the session he will be able to keep the weapon. If he does not, it will be sent to his relatives with the rest of his possessions."

"Enough talk Mac, try to kill me." The sergeant made a halfhearted lunge with the blade and Lewis contemptuously swatted the knife out of his hand.

"If you can't do better than that Mac, I'm really going to hurt you," Lewis snarled. Stung by the contempt, Mac came in low, hard and fast. He feinted with the blade and aimed a kick at the balls. Lewis blocked the kick with his hip and the next thing the sergeant knew he was on the ground with the knife sticking a quarter inch in his throat.

"Much better Mac," he said, and repeated his moves against the sergeant in slow motion. For the next two hours Lewis had the sergeant try his best to kill him and then repeated his counter moves. At the end of the session, Mac was soaked with blood and sweat while Lewis was unmarked in his clean, pressed fatigues. Mac handed the knife to Lewis, who shook his head. "Keep it Mac, you earned it."

It was the beginning of a love affair between Lewis and the 101st Airborne that would last for over forty years. Lewis admired the pride and toughness of the men of an outfit that never quit, and the men admired Lewis for the same reasons. Mac and Lewis were first sergeants in different companies, but throughout the war they always managed to get together for beer and bullshit.

The 101st Airborne Division was to be dropped into France, make contact with the French resistance, and destroy roads, bridges and German communications then link up with the invasion force landing at Utah beach. They were to be parachuted into a field the night before the invasion along with the supplies for the French. The night of the operation, the weather deteriorated and the drop zones were hidden by clouds. The Germans had flooded the fields in anticipation of an airborne assault and many of the paratroops, hampered by their heavy equipment, were drowned. Other units were dropped far from their targets, and the confusion of the Allies was only equaled by the confusion of the German high command. Lewis's stick was one of the few units to hit their correct zone, but he landed in a shallow pond and got stuck in the mud. The enthusiastic French grabbed his chute and pulled him, face down through the duck shit, to dry land. The guns and supplies were quickly loaded into waiting trucks. The leader of the resistance in Normandy was a French woman. She was called the 'black widow' by the few Germans that had survived her bite, and was sought after by the Gestapo, and the French quasi Gestapo called the Milca.

MARIE VASQUEZ / 1944-1990

7

Her real name was Marie Vasquez, and she was the result of a brief union between a Spanish pimp and a French prostitute. After she was born, her mother gave up the life of a prostitute and became the owner of a successful nightclub. Marie was a true hermaphrodite and had male genitalia and female ovaries, an obvious fact ignored by her mother who hated men. Maria grew into a beautiful 'woman' and became a famous female impersonator with a soft contralto voice that she could change into a deep masculine chuckle. Her songs and skits lampooning Hitler and Goring delighted French audiences but infuriated the Nazis.

When France fell to the Germans, she was rounded up with the other 'undesirables' to be sent to a concentration camp. A young German guard fell in love with her and took her to a storeroom. When he reached into her panties he stiffened with shock, and then stiffened again with his own knife in his kidney. As he lay on the floor, writhing in agony, she calmly put on his uniform, cut his throat and walked out of the jail to join the resistance. Lewis had been getting mixed signals from this beautiful woman, and when 'she' told him that she was a 'he' Lewis did not believe it, so she showed him her credentials.

Much later, after they had become close friends, Lewis asked her that if she loved women and not men, why not drop the woman act and just be a man. Marie looked at him sadly.

"I was raised by my mother to be a girl. I never undressed around other women, and never dated a boy in high school. I was kissed by a man after a college dance and it almost made me vomit." She looked at Lewis, trying to give him an honest answer, and finally said, "Lewis, I am just comfortable as a woman."

The weapons and supplies were unloaded in a barn a few miles from a crossroad leading from the small town of Carentan to the invasion site of Utah Beach. The objective of the paratroops was to destroy the German artillery that defended the landing site. Marie, using her 'maiden in distress' look and a broken bike, stopped a German staff car, and calmly shot the occupants with her machine pistol that she had in a basket. While they were waiting, two more trucks driven by partisans arrived with 40 more lost men from the 101st. The senior officer of the group decided to send the Lewis and a driver with the staff car to recon the artillery positions. Lewis wiped the blood from a major's uniform and Dave, the driver, picked out one with a good fit.

When they arrived at the first artillery bunker, Lewis looked furious at the slipshod condition of the huge weapons, the absence of infantry support for the guns and the general lackadaisical attitude of the men and officers.

"If Field Marshall Rommel was here he would have you all sent to the Russian front," he yelled at the terrified officers.

He was told that a battalion of infantry was due to arrive the next day, and the mortified officers assured him that the guns would be ready for the Field Marshall's inspection. Lewis returned to the staff car, got in and they drove away. Dave, who did not speak a word of German, started laughing.

"Sarge, you are so full of horseshit." Lewis, who was still pumped with adrenalin, said,

"Corporal, you have just witnessed one of the great impromptu performances of the war. The German is very orderly and sees what he expects to see. Those officers knew that the guns were unkempt and their men soft and lazy. They also expected an ass chewing. If I had given them a compliment, they would have relaxed and started asking questions about things I know nothing about. As Hitler himself once said, 'the bigger the lie the greater the belief.'"

When they arrived back at the crossroads over 200 paratroops had straggled in. A newly arrived colonel had taken command and Lewis briefed him and the other officers. Marie and her men were sent towards Caen to blow up any bridges that would slow down the German infantry. The rest of the 101st would be ferried to a jump-off point a mile from the artillery and prepare for a dawn attack. The colonel told Lewis and Dave to get out of the German uniforms before they were shot. They were to go ahead in the staff car and guide the men to their positions. The attack would begin just before dawn when the invasion force was not visible.

The Arabs say that it is dawn when a white thread can be distinguished from a black thread. In the faint light of dawn, the Germans were mesmerized by the sight of thousands of ships off the coast of Normandy. The 101st hit the coastal batteries just before the massive naval bombardment began. The German guns were protected by concrete bunkers over ten feet thick. The paratroops only had hand grenades and satchel charges, but without infantry protection the gunners were quickly killed or taken prisoner. In a few hours the 101st linked up with the first units from Utah Beach.

The rumor spread among the men of the 101st about the sergeant that could impersonate a German officer, and even mimic the mannerisms of Hitler or Goring. This came to the attention of a colonel named William Donavan, commander of the newly formed OSS. Donavan asked Lewis to work for him behind enemy lines in France and Germany, gathering intelligence and working with the resistance. Lewis declined, but told Donavan that he ought to recruit Marie Vasquez.

"Just don't try to grope her," he added. Marie became the crown jewel in Donovan's shadow empire, and was given the Legion of Honor at the end of the war.

VINNIE

8

The 101st pressed northward through France, and Lewis's unit was used mostly for scouting and reconnaissance. It was commanded by Lieutenant George Major, who had been a history teacher in civilian life. They were an odd couple, the huge young sergeant and the small thin lieutenant. Lewis loved history and they would spend hours discussing German history and wondering how it was possible for such a brilliant people to be led by a group of Nazi thugs. It was a tight knit unit and new recruits were ignored until they had proven themselves in combat. Corporal Vincent, 'Vinnie,' Schapiro was a cocky 24-year-old recruit from New York who had replaced a veteran that lost a foot when he stepped on a mine. Vinnie regaled the men with his experiences with the mob and how a judge gave him a choice of the army or prison. Vinnie proved to be a real asset to the unit as he could steal anything. He could open any lock with the skill of a magician, 'borrow' jeeps from other units, acquire new socks by the bale and booze by the case. Lieutenant Major turned a blind eye to these activities, but always shared in the spoils. In return Lewis taught him how to stay alive. How to spot the best place for a sniper 'hide', the most likely places for mines and booby traps, and most importantly, how to kill Germans.

Vinnie had one glaring fault. His stealing included items from the men of his own unit. Lewis told him to knock it off or he would pound him into small pieces. Vinnie rose to the challenge and blatantly stole all of Lewis's dry socks. Lewis called him out and they faced off the next morning. Most of the company was betting on Lewis, but when Vinnie took off his shirt the odds shortened considerably. Six foot tall with a chest like a beer keg, he was an awesome sight.

"Corporal, you can take a bust to private and avoid a trip to the hospital," Vinnie sneered and charged. The fight was over in a few seconds, and Vinnie lay in the mud with a fractured arm and a broken jaw.

A few days later the chastened corporal reported back to Lieutenant Major. He had sneaked out of the hospital with his jaw wired shut and his arm in a cast.

"I can reassign you to a different company corporal," and when Vinnie shook his head no, the lieutenant added, "but the decision is up to Sergeant Lewis." Vinnie walked into Lewis's tent and stood silently in front of his erstwhile foe. Lewis looked at him with a grin.

"Welcome home, Vinnie." The corporal turned away so

that Lewis could not see the tears in his eyes.

The battered company was pulled off line and given R & R in the newly liberated Paris. The city had wildly welcomed the French battalion that had first marched in followed by the Americans and British. The MP's were thick on the streets to prevent any exuberant soldiers from destroying the city, but most of the men just wanted to eat, drink and sleep. In a few days many of the units had found small bars where they could gather with their friends and get away from the officers and MP's. Lewis, Vinnie and four others were playing poker in a small bar. Lewis had the reputation of being the worst poker player in the company. He always put on his 'poker face' when he was bluffing and relaxed when he had a good hand.

Lewis was losing as usual and Vinnic was winning as usual, when the noisy bar became very quiet. Lewis looked up and saw the most beautiful woman in Paris walking towards their table. It was Marie, dressed to the nines in a shear black dress, six inch heels and a huge smile. She walked up to Lewis, who was at a loss whether to kiss her cheek or shake hands. Marie wrapped her arms around and gave him a long lingering kiss on the lips. Lewis introduced her to his friends.

"Men, this is Marie Vasquez. She was leader of the resistance in Normandy and has killed more Krauts than typhoid."

Marie sat down and started playing, kidding and laughing with the players, who were concentrating on her breasts instead of the cards. Soon the other players were cleaned out except for Vinnie who had recovered most of his wits. Vinnie looked at her across the table and said,

"Marie lets up the stakes with a little strip poker." Lewis was appalled. *Christ* he thought, *that is all I need, Marie with her dick hanging out. After that kiss I'll be the goat of the whole division.* Marie looked at him, reading his mind and enjoying his discomfort. She grinned at Vinnie.

"Sounds good to me. Let's start with five stud."

Vinnie won the first two hands and Marie lost her shoes. Marie won the next three and Vinnie lost his shoes and a sock. The next several hands were evenly split with Vinnie losing his shirt and Marie her brassiere. She took it off without removing her dress, much to the disappointment of the onlookers. The next hand Vinnie had a pair of kings showing and Marie showed an ace high nothing. Vinnie was sweating, while Marie was cool as ice.

"All or nothing?" she asked. Vinnie shook his head no, and turned over a duce and Marie an ace for the win. Vinnie won the next hand and Marie raised an eyebrow to Lewis and slowly removed her dress revealing her beautiful breasts. Both players were down to their underwear, and Lewis was ready to bolt for the door. The bar was packed solid, and the street was crowded with soldiers that had picked up on the action. Marie called for a fresh deck and Vinnie smiled at her and said,

"Dear Marie," let's cut to the chase and cut the cards for the win." Marie thought for a moment, and then replied,

"On one condition, if I lose you will give me a great big kiss." Vinnie agreed and shuffled the cards, then extending the deck to Marie, he said "Ladies first." Lewis closed his eyes and thought, *"Well, if she loses, Vinnie and I will be in the same boat."* Marie reached for the deck and cut a three of hearts. The crowd roared and Vinnie raised his fist and whooped for joy. He reached for the deck and cut—a duce of diamonds. Shock followed by resignation crossed his face. Finally a voice shouted from the silent crowd, "take it off Vinnie, you dumb wop." Vinnie climbed on the table and with great panache began slowly peeling off his shorts to imaginary strip music. He was twirling his dick and doing a credible bump and grind, and for the grand finale he bent over and mooned the whole crowd.

Marie managed to get dressed sitting down thereby hiding the bulge in her panties. She stood up and told the men that she and Lewis had some things to discuss and thanked Vinnie for an interesting evening. They walked to a black Mercedes touring car, got in and rode in silence. Finally Lewis said,

"Marie, if you had dropped your drawers I would have shit my pants." Marie started to giggle, and then shook with laughter, and soon Lewis was laughing with her. Marie managed to gasp, "You should have seen your face when I cut that three" and went back into convulsions. Marie wiped the tears from her eyes and reached over and took his hand.

"My dear Lewis, I kissed you tonight just to make you

squirm, but I love you like a brother, and not like a woman. I love women because I am a man in a woman's body, and it's very difficult for me to attract a woman,. I come on to a woman and she rejects me as a lesbian. If she is a lesbian, she rejects me as a man. All of my relationships are with whores who do not care what you are as long as you can pay. I have talked to a doctor about this and he told me I could get my breasts removed, but I am really afraid. Basically, my dear friend, I am well and truly fucked." Lewis was silent, mulling over her litany of hopelessness. Finally he said,

"Marie you are truly a unique person in this world. You have more courage, class and style than anyone I have ever known. You will find a mate; of this I am absolutely certain." Marie laid her head on his chest and the tears fell like rain.

The Mercedes dropped them off at a large stone house, but before they entered Marie pulled him aside.

"Donovan is waiting for you", she said. "He wants you and I to do some work in Belgium, near a town called Baaschtnech". This was the second time Lewis met the legendary spymaster and he was still concerned that Donovan would ask him to leave his unit to go waltzing around in Germany, blowing up bridges and the like. Bill Donovan, Medal of Honor winner, friend of Roosevelt and Churchill, America's spymaster and a superb poker player read him like a book.

"Lewis and Marie two of the toughest, smartest people in Europe", he said, poring on the snake oil. "I would like you to work for me for a week or ten days, on a matter that may well affect the war. Near that unpronounceable town in Belgium, we are hearing rumors that the Krauts are massing Panzer Divisions. That is not a real good place for armor and I doubt that the Krauts are stupid enough to attack, but we need to check it out."

"How are we going to get near those divisions without getting shot?" Lewis asked.

"Simple" Donovan replied. "Marie knows the local chief of the underground in that area. When you get to Baaschtnech she will contact him, and you can walk to the German lines."

"An Airborne Sergeant and a blond bombshell, it sounds like a good plan." Lewis said sarcastically.

"Well there will need to be a few refinements" Donovan said. "You will have to wear a German officer's uniform, say a Colonel, and Marie would be your aid We would cut and dye her hair, and bind up those uh, those beautiful breasts" he said with a slight blush, "and voila the perfect aid or driver." Lewis looked at Marie, and then said to Donovan,

"Give us an hour to think about it," and they went into the kitchen and thought about Donovan's proposal. Finally Lewis broke the silence.

"You know Marie, if the Krauts catch you in a German uniform they'll probably cut off your tits and stuff your cock and balls in your mouth." Marie gave him a cool haughty look that reminded him of Vinnie and the strip poker game.

41

"I have lived with that possibility for years" she said, "and they will probably cut off your dick and hang you with it."

"That's the downside alright, "Lewis admitted, "Then where are the benefits? "If that madman turns his army loose there will be a lot of dead men, including our friends," Marie replied. "So let's tell the man with the plan that it's on."

After showing his new orders to the battalion CO at Reims where the 101st was being held in reserve, they drove towards the front lines in the shiny black Mercedes that Donovan had reluctantly loaned them.

"Don't scratch the paint job, "he admonished, "It's the only new Mercedes in France." Lewis wore his regular uniform, and Marie was outfitted as a corporal. Her hair was black with a military haircut, and her breasts were flattened with gauze and tape. *It sure changed her appearance alright,* Lewis thought. *From a beautiful woman to a pretty boy.*

"Half the faggots in France will be chasing you," he remarked."By the way, how do you say Baaschtnech in German?" .

"It's Baaschtnech in German", she replied. "In French it's Bastogne"

BASTOGNE

9

As they drove north they could hear the distant rumble of artillery, and a few miles later a southbound convoy of 1st Army trucks passed them loaded with wounded. The further north they drove the more congested the road became with beat up, tired soldiers. The jeeps had stretchers on the hood and wounded piled in the back. Finally, a few miles from Bastogne, they were stopped by a wild-eyed captain, who told him to get out of the Mercedes as it was needed to evacuate several high-ranking officers. When Lewis showed him his orders and refused, the captain pulled out his .45 and told him to get out or be killed. Lewis got out and with his pistol still pointing at Lewis, the captain slid into the driver's seat. Marie promptly drove her K bar under his jaw and into his brain. Lewis took the pistol from the dead man's hand, stuck it in the wound under his jaw and pulled the trigger. He put the weapon back into the captain's hand and remarked,

"Looks like suicide to me."

Further up the road Lewis spotted a young Catholic priest carrying a soldier without a foot with a blind man hanging onto his shoulder. He told the priest and the soldiers to get in. He corralled three more wounded, and told the man that had one good arm and both legs to turn the car around and head for Reims. Marie pulled their equipment out of the trunk, throwing the duffle bags with the German uniforms in the ditch, and they started walking towards Bastogne.

"You didn't tell the driver where to return Bill's car."

"Fuck him" Lewis replied and they marched on, two going north, hundreds heading south.

Marie carried her German machine pistol, and an M1 with four clips. Lewis carried his big sniper rifle that he had picked up in Reims and a box of .50 caliber ammo. They finally arrived in Bastogne, where a harried major was rounding up cooks, clerks and the walking wounded and giving them empty rifles, telling them to get ammo off the dead. Lewis asked him where he wanted them to go. He noticed Lewis's Screaming Eagle patch and said,

"Where the hell is the rest of your outfit?" Lewis just shrugged, and the disgusted Major pointed towards the sound of increasing gunfire.

They found a position on the line behind a frozen log. The two men on the right were lying in a shallow foxhole; a corporal grinned and told them to save their ammo. Lewis peered through the scope at Germans. They all had white snow suits and none had rank patches showing. At a thousand yards he zeroed in on a tank with its 88 mm cannon pointed at their position, and pulled the trigger. The big gun was not vented or silenced. The blast made everyone on the line jump and the German tank commander disappeared.

"Jesus," said the corporal, and then pointed at a machine gun that was out of M1 range. "See if you can pop those guys." Lewis obliged and killed all three, with three quick shots. With the keen-eyed corporal spotting, Lewis started picking off Germans, including an officer with binoculars at least one hundred yards behind the tank.

That night the 101st arrived and started filling up the thin line. The Germans welcomed them with artillery and 88 fire, the air bursts raining down shrapnel and tree tops. Lewis and Marie clawed a shallow trench under their log with bleeding fingers. *My Kingdom for a shovel* Lewis thought, as the shells plowed up the ground around them. Marie looked at him and winked.

The artillery fire stopped and the Germans came surging forward. Suddenly the field that the infantry had to cross was lit up by a star shell and the American line started killing Germans with relish. Marie fired her M1 until the rifle was empty, then she picked her pistol and started firing short bursts at the closing enemy. The .50 was too slow and Lewis said, "To hell with it." Throwing his big gun aside, he picked up the empty M1, jumped over the log and bayoneted a German sergeant. The German veterans were tough and it was a melee of stabbing, kicking and gouging. Lewis caught a bayonet in the shoulder and when the German tried to pull it out Marie stabbed him in the side with her K Bar. The fighting along the line was fierce until the remaining Germans backed away, both sides exhausted and with empty weapons. Lewis had a deep slash across his forehead and his eyes were blind with blood, his shoulder was throbbing. Marie did not have a scratch. She picked up a bag from a dead medic and patched up Lewis's head wound, then went down the line helping the wounded, calming them with her soft woman's voice.

The weather cleared the next day and two C47s were able to drop some ammo and rations. Lewis and Marie rejoined Fox Company. Vinnie saw Marie and she knew the jig was up. His jaw dropped.

"What the hell are you doing here?" So she had to explain to him, and the rest of the men about her OSS connection, the disguise and the aborted scouting expedition. Marie went behind a tree, cut off her bindings, massaged her sore breasts, and walked back to the group with a sexy jiggle. The corporal who had been spotting for Lewis shook his head in admiration.

"You are one tough lady," he said, and the rest of the company loudly agreed.

The fighting see-sawed back and forth until Christmas, when the German units made a final desperate attempt to seize the town and its vital crossroads. Since Marie knew as much about treating battle wounds, as inflicting them, she worked as a medic. She was fearless and the men treated her like the Virgin Mary. Lewis went back to work with the Corporal from the 1st Army unit that had the keen eyes. Lewis started training him as a sniper. Corporal John T. Hillman was a natural, and soon he and Lewis were splitting the duties of the shooter and the spotter. A few days after Christmas, Patton's 4th Armored Division arrived and the siege of Bastogne was over.

As the fighting stopped around Bastogne Marie spent most of her time in the field hospital. The medics and doctors admired her care and deep affection for her men, and were eager to teach her their hard won skills. A jeep pulled up to division headquarters and General Patton of the Third Army dismounted. General McAuliffe, Commander of the 101st Division, walked over and they exchanged salutes. Patton heard the sound of a woman laughing, looked up and saw Marie talking to an Italian looking Corporal. He turned to General McAuliffe.

"Since when have we had women paratroops?"

"She's with Donovan's bunch. She got trapped here with us and joined the fight. We were glad to have her," McAuliffe explained. "She's a French citizen, so I can't put her in for anything, but I'm going to see if Ike can have de Gaul give her recognition for her work here."

"Good idea Mac," said the general. "Women belong in hospitals where the men know they are safe, and not running around getting shot at." General McAuliffe smiled and said nothing.

JEANETTE

10

"How about it Marie?" Vinnie said. "We could borrow a jeep and run to town for a few beers and a little dancing." Marie gave him a cool appraising look that she knew always made him nervous. Lewis had told her that Vinnie had married early and forcefully, having been unwise enough to impregnate the Capo's daughter, and had a two year old daughter of his own. His philandering never seemed to bother him and he tried to get into Maries pants whenever Lewis was not around. Marie was tempted to drop her drawers and give him a good look, but the shock would probably kill him, she giggled at the thought and was saved from having to reject Vinnie by a courier handing her a message. It was from Donovan's office, and she said to Vinnie, "got to go" and went to pack.

When she arrived at headquarters in Paris, Donovan's first words were, "Where is my Mercedes?"

She pecked him on the cheek and said, "Nice to see you

too Bill." *He always colors a bit when I kiss him on the cheek* she mused. *It must be his puritanical upbringing conflicting with his admiration for my tits.*

"I hope you enjoyed your vacation," he grumbled, "but it's time to get back to work.

The work he outlined to Marie promised to be a loser for the OSS. Bills counterintelligence Deputy was almost certain that they had an Abwehr mole in the agency that had been in place since operation Overlord. The deputy had been feeding her a few tidbits of lies mixed in with the truth, and the Germans had reacted to the truth. A few fresh male faces had tried getting close, but the young woman had rejected their advances. Bill wanted Marie to have a shot.

"What do you want me to do if I find out she is an agent in the Abwehr?" Donovan looked her in the eye,

"Find out how the information is being transmitted, and anything else important, then kill her."

The young woman's name was Jeanette Dubois and was a French citizen from a wealthy Parisian family. Marie was given an office near Donovan's. She was too well known to pose as some new recruit. Her first encounter with Jeanette was in the powder room, where they exchanged a few polite greetings. Marie didn't push it, as agents working in the heart of an enemy intelligence agency, were extremely cautious.

Marie was sitting, having coffee in the lunchroom and casually looked in Jeanette's direction and saw the girl stiffen and her eyes widen slightly with a fear she could not hide. Marie stood up and turned to go and saw that the object of the girls eyes was a tall handsome agent that was sometimes used as a 'Raven' to seduce women in an enemy agency.

The next day Marie called the agent and they met in a coffee shop.

"How's your acting ability?"she asked.

"I've got to be a good actor to seduce some of those hags for the good of the country." he said eying her cleavage.

They worked out a plan and two days later, in the lunch-room, the employees were shocked by menace in Marie's voice.

"Get out of my sight or I'll cut off your balls." The agent did not have to act, and turned around and fled the room. Marie finished her lunch and walked out of the silent lunchroom.

Marie was a bit uncomfortable with the results of her staged drama. Jeanette thawed immediately and her eyes were filled with admiration that turned to love as the days passed. Marie carefully fed her pieces of information and nothing happened. Another week went by and Marie was starting to think that the Deputy of Counterintelligence was sniffing at the wrong hole. Another unintended consequence was that the girl was coming on strong and told Marie that she wanted to go to bed with her. Donovan decided to give it one last shot and gave Marie a piece of intelligence that would be priceless to the Germans. Marie left the information in an unsealed envelope on her desk where Jeanette would see it and went to Bills office for an hour. When she returned, the envelope had been moved slightly. Another week went by and nothing happened.

Donovan called off the operation. Bill, the Deputy and Marie all agreed that the girl was clean. Marie was leaving for England to work with British intelligence for six months and was packing when she heard a knock at the door. Jeanette stood there the tears streaming down her face. The girl jumped into Marie's arms and gave her a deep, full tongued kiss. Marie felt a surge of desire, and reached under the girls blouse and squeezed a rock-hard nipple.

And suddenly a cold knowledge of the truth crushed the tumescence in her groin and the desire in her heart. Jeanette had not passed the information to the Abwehr because of her love for her, Marie, her protector. *And now my dear, your judge, jury and executioner.*

Marie returned the kiss, avoiding the hands reaching for her groin and guiding them expertly to her own breasts. She led the girl to the bedroom, laid her down on the bed and slowly undressed her, caressing her with tongue and hands. Marie started gently asking her questions, and Jeanette answered with almost hypnotic truthfulness. Soon the information poured out without probing. Lies, deceits and gilt came out behind a dam of fear that had been gnawing at her for years. Her very wealthy parents had used her to mine information to prolong the war for a cabal of industrialists, and not necessarily to help the Nazis. Their greed had caused the death of uncounted millions as the war raged on. Marie stroked the girl to orgasm, and then repeated the process until she was ready again. Marie undressed and entered her, thrusting and kissing her until the girl was limp and spent. She lay next to her and stroked her hair and face.

Just before she fell asleep, Jeanette put her hand on Marie's penis and said,

"I love you daddy," and fell asleep.

"I love you too child." Marie whispered, the tears streaming down her face. It will all be over soon my love, and Marie got out of bed, dressed and made a call.

The needle slid smoothly into the vein and the colorless fluid entered the heart and the young woman died without waking up.

The fire raged through the mansion, killing Jeanette's parents, but not before her father named the names of families and industries of the cabal in five countries. Under the questioning of Donovan's team of expert inquisitors, Jeanette's mother died of a heart attack. Jeanette's remains were cremated along with her parent's in the conflagration.

Marie told Donovan that she was taking some time off, and the wise old spymaster told her to go ahead even though he needed her in England. She drove into Germany and tracked down the 101st Headquarters Company, then hitched a ride to Lewis's recon unit. Lewis looked up from a pile of rifle parts and grinned at her. "Hi kid, what's going on?" Marie felt a weight lifting from her heart. Lewis looked deep into her eyes, the smile fading. *Something is really wrong. She's hurting bad.*

He wordlessly took her hand and they drove to a village inn that hadn't been touched by the war. On a small veranda, looking out over the quiet countryside, Marie poured out the tale of the sordid business that was tearing her apart.

"My God Lewis," she was used by everyone, like a piece of toilet paper," she said between deep, choking sobs, "And Marie," she sneered, "her great protector, pumped her dry, fucked her like her father did, and killed her."

Marie slowly stopped sobbing, and they both sat silently for an hour. Marie was lost in thought.

Lewis is the most honest man that I have ever known. I may not like what he will tell me but it will be the truth. Lewis looked up.

"Why did you fuck her when she had already told you everything?" Marie started to say something then stopped. *Good question, was lust a part of it, or pity, or…*

"I was trying to comfort her Lewis, and that is why I killed her. I couldn't let Bills men have her. She had been used enough, and I put an end to her suffering."

"Donovan ever ask you anything about what you did?" Lewis asked.

"Nope." she replied.

"If he ever does tell him to take a flying fuck at a rolling doughnut." Marie laughed for the first time since she stuck the needle into Jeanette's arm."

EAGLES NEST

11

The American advance shifted towards the German-Austrian border where it was believed the Germans would make their final stand. The 101st moved cautiously up the narrow road leading towards Hitler's famous redoubt called the Eagle's Nest. They crawled through a tunnel and stopped at an elevator cut into solid rock. They heard the elevator coming down, and the men of Fox Company stepped back, covering the door ready to fire. They relaxed when a startled young woman emerged, carrying a heavy satchel loaded with documents. The woman pleaded with the soldiers not to shoot her and the few remaining clerks and secretaries at the Eagle's Nest. The elevator ride was three hundred feet to the top with the men half expecting an ambush at the end. With no enemy in sight, the troops quickly rounded up the occupants and called up the rest of the company.

Lewis arrived with Lieutenant Major, and acting as an interpreter, asked a young clerk the location of Goring's famous wine cellar. Most of the men relaxed, sipping expensive wine and smoking exotic cigars. A few intrepid souls walked through the labyrinth of tunnels and rooms carved in the solid rock under Hitler's redoubt. In one of the tunnels the men found the name of a woman carved in the cold rock by a Russian slave. "Nadia," a monument of a dead soldier to a lost love.

The company was in no hurry to leave the Eagle's Nest, with its fine wine and excellent food. A German chef fed the men like kings and Lewis and Vinnie started exploring the vast structure. Vinnie was an experienced thief, and like most of his ilk had an eye for secret hiding places. Most of the rooms and tunnels were left in disarray by the fleeing Germans. Vinnie was looking in a huge stone fireplace and spotted a slight tilt in one of the heavy steel andirons. He called Lewis over and together they lifted the andiron and the stone to which it was bolted.

They could barely lift it, but when they did they found a small steel box in a hollow cut in the stone underneath. Vinnie snapped open the lock, and they found a handful of jewelry and a manuscript in German. While Vinnie divided the spoils, Lewis read the manuscript. It was a detailed description of the hiding places of the art treasures looted by the Nazis. Lewis wanted to give the jewelry to the Army, but Vinnie argued that it should be a finder's fee for the discovery of such a valuable document. Lewis reluctantly agreed, and they pocketed the loot. They gave the manuscript to Majors, and Lewis explained why it was so valuable. The lieutenant was so excited by the find he did not notice the guilty look on his sergeant's face. He sent the manuscript by courier to Captain Farmer, who headed up the "Monuments Men," the team designated to recover stolen art and other treasure. He received a commendation from General Eisenhower, and a promotion to captain.

The war ended for Lewis and the 101st in 1945, and the division was deactivated and sent home. The 101st was the most decorated division that had survived the war, with its men receiving numerous medals and citations. Lewis, Vinnie and others got their Silver Stars pinned on them by Ike and Lewis got his third Purple Heart…for a very minor wound.

MARY ANN BROWN

12

Mary Ann Brown sometimes wished that her aunt Ida was a bit more like her mother and not quite so vocal about the rights of women. But Ida didn't stop with women's rights, she protested almost everything. Her favorite target in Orophino was the River Bend Whorehouse. The Clearwater river was the highway for the massive log drives from the high woods to the mills in Lewiston. In the middle of thousands of logs roiling in the turbulent water were the Wannigans. These were log rafts with cabins where the drivers ate and slept on the long drive from the woods to the mills. The 'cat house' was located on a bend in the river near Orophino. Some of the men would race across the rolling logs, pike poles in hand, into the cat house, do their business without taking off their caulk boots, and catch the drive on the other side.

Jim Wilson was the Bull of the Woods, the man responsible for getting the logs from the decks to the mills. In the upper reaches of the Clearwater the log jams would have to be cleared with peavy's or with dynamite. Either way Jim got the job done. He would never send in a man to do a dangerous job that he wouldn't do himself.

He was walking back to his small home with a bag of groceries, when Ida spotted him and pounced like a hawk.

"You let those animals loose on those poor women. Why can't you keep them penned up on the river?"

"Well mam, it's pretty hard times right now and the girls make good money from my drivers." Jim said mildly. An exasperated voice behind him said,

"For Gods sake Ida, leave the poor man alone, and lets get going. Ben's nose is getting red". Jim turned around and saw a very pretty young woman with a small boy on her hip. Their eyes locked and Jim thought *oh boy*. Mary saw the old familiar look and colored slightly. She had been celibate for almost two years and didn't like the feeling. The obvious interest of the big tough looking man was like a breath of spring. The boy reached out for him and said, "Big." and the "Bull of the Woods" was hooked.

On December 7th 1941 Japanese forces bombed Pearl Harbor and the next day Jim Wilson Joined the Marines Mary Ann Wilson and Ida returned to Oregon. While Mary was working in a munitions factory, Ida stayed in Cottage Grove and raised little Ben. When Mary learned of the formation of the Women Air force Service Pilots training program, she immediately volunteered and was accepted. She was first in her class and spent the next three years ferrying B-24 bombers to bases in Texas and California.

Jim landed with the Marines on Guadalcanal and quickly solved the problems of Japanese fortifications the same way he removed log jams. He was promoted to platoon sergeant and had attained the rank of master sergeant by the time the 5th Division landed at Okinawa. While Jim was slogging through the hell of Okinawa, Mary was ferrying B-24s. Like all new equipment, the planes had a few bugs and one of them was fatal. In the subsequent crash, the copilot was killed and Mary barely escaped the burning plane.

Neither Jim nor Mary received each others letters. They had been automatically re-routed to Washington and classified. Officially Mary did not exist in the military as she was considered a civilian employee. Ida was having a tough time raising Ben. The boy asked her very pointed questions and when she tried evasion, Ben would give her a disgusted look and check the encilopedia.

When Jim came home, Mary quit the Air Force and joined him in Cottage Grove. They spent their nights catching up on the four years apart and the four years of abstinence. It wasn't long before Mary was pregnant, and both she and Ida prayed for a girl. Ben was an eight-year-old handful for Ida but Jim treated him like a man. Ben needed a father to guide and love him and he found both in Jim Wilson.

When Lewis arrived home after a seven year absence, it wasn't very long before he called the Wilsons. Jim invited him over for dinner, and Mary was a bit nervous about Jim meeting her old lover. She shouldn't have worried as the bond between the two noncoms was instantaneous. Lewis hugged Mary.

"God Jim, you sure robbed the cradle. She still looks like a high school kid.

"Yup, and if you'd caught up with her old Emeritus would have given you both a formal wedding…with a white shotgun.

"Ben, this your uncle Lewis."Lewis looked into the bright green eyes of a boy who was much older than his age. He hid the pain in his heart, *This could have been my kid, but Mary's right, I'm a better uncle than a father.*

"With any luck you'll grow up to be as pretty as I am." Ben grinned, "Only in your dreams uncle, only in your dreams." They walked into the yard to fire up the grill, joshing Ben and joking about the green officers they had known. Mary watched them with her son with tears in her eyes. Tears of happiness or sadness, she didn't know which. .

KOREA / 1946-1953

13

Lewis did not want to leave the Army. He asked around and found out through the sergeant's grapevine that a Captain Hausman was being sent to Korea to help train the new Korean army. He found Hausman and asked him if he could use an experienced sergeant. "Damned right." Hausman said, and they agreed to meet after a few months leave in the States.

It seemed that the whole town of Cottage Grove was out to welcome him as he stepped off the plane at the Eugene airport. He felt like the prodigal son, surrounded by his crying parents and brothers. Most of his friends, many of them veterans, shook his hand and his old girlfriends gave him hugs and kisses as the crowd cheered.

Back home Lewis gave his family the souvenirs that he had picked up in Germany and France. He gave his mother a diamond studded crucifix from Goring's hoard. An Iron Cross from a dead German and a machine pistol from a live one went to his father. His older brother, got an SS belt buckle and small gold bust of Hitler went to his younger brother. He pinned his Silver Star on his dad and the three Purple Hearts on the kid's. He gave the wives two bottles of French perfume, almost cleaning out his stash.

Over the next several weeks Lewis drove around town in his brother's old pickup, talking to friends and visiting the Wilsons. When Lewis said he was going to Korea to train soldiers, Jim gave him a thoughtful look.

"You know that the Japs really hammered the Koreans. They used them as labor to build their island fortifications and thousands died of disease or starvation. The women were used as 'love' slaves for the soldiers and Korea was used as a rice basket to feed the military. They occupied the country as a 'protectorate' since 1910 and the economy is a shambles."

The next day, thinking of Jim's words about the Koreans, Lewis drove to the Eugene library looking for books on Korean history, language and culture and came up empty. He went to the University library with the same results; finally in a used bookstore he found an English-Korean dictionary and a history book. He phoned the University and asked if they had an oriental studies program. He gave the head of the department his name and a brief explanation of his interest in Korea. He was met at the University by a striking young Asian woman named Cindy Chu.

"Most people call me Cindy Lou" she said. They met the head of the Oriental Studies program, Professor Frank

Connors, who came around his desk to shake hands with Lewis.

"If you are the same Lewis Sergeant that's in the papers it's a real honor to meet you." Lewis was a bit uncomfortable with the honor part but asked the professor for any help he could give him on Korea.

"Cindy is bilingual in English and Korean. Her parents are Korean and taught Cindy the language. She is more than willing to help you with the language and cultural studies." Lewis cocked an eyebrow at Cindy, who smiled and nodded her agreement.

Cindy Chu proved to be an excellent teacher and a hard taskmaster, but Lewis's gift for languages astonished her. After a week, Cindy invited him to her home and they sat around the kitchen table with her parents talking in Korean. Cindy's mother giggled at his mistakes, but noticed that Lewis never made the same one twice. During their breaks at the University they chatted with other students, and Lewis was surprised at the number of them that were adherents of Marxism. Back in the Yu household, Lewis told the family that Stalin had killed as many people as Hitler, and that the Communists would turn Korea into a prison if they conquered the South. Cindy's parents looked at each other, and finally confessed that they had been getting disturbing letters from their friends and families in the North. Since Cindy could not read or write Korean, this news came as a shock to her.

One evening as they were finishing their studies, Cindy

put her hand on his knee.

"Lewis, why haven't you made a pass at me?" He looked at her and shrugged, "You never gave me any encouragement"

"I am not an 'inscrutable oriental', and besides the man is supposed to make the first advance," she said primly.

"Consider it done and he put his arm around her waist and kissed her. Cindy led him to a small conference room and locked the door. They sat on the couch, kissing, exploring and removing each other's clothes. They made love for hours, and only stopped when a janitor rattled the door. When they had dressed, Cindy took his hand and smiled, "Thank you for a wonderful evening, Lewis" and he smiled back and said,

"The pleasure was all mine." In the short time that they had left, Lewis taught her the French arts of oral sex, and she taught him the nuances of the Korean language, including some words that were not in his Korean / English dictionary. When it was time for him to leave, she did not accompany him to the airport. She said that she would feel awkward around his family.

JOE CHANG / 1946

14

In 1946, officers and men from the U.S. Army were sent to Korea as advisors. The unit was called KMAG for Korean Military Advisory Group. They were sent to train a Korean police force called a constabulary to keep order in the newly liberated country. Among the contingent was a Japanese American or Nisi. His name was Joseph Chang and was from the 442nd Regimental Combat Team. He and Lewis were both NCO advisors. When they met for the first time, Lewis snapped to attention and saluted Sergeant Chang, one of the few living Medal of Honor winners of the 442nd. This all-Japanese unit fought in Europe, and was the most decorated small unit in American history.

Volunteers for the Advisory Group were hard to find, as Korea was considered a hardship post. The country had been occupied by the Japanese since 1910, and had served as a "rice bowl" and a source of labor for the Japanese empire. The economy was weak, there was little industry, and the military was almost non-existent. It soon became apparent to the advisors that this police force needed to be trained along military lines, and to become the core of a Korean army.

Lewis was assigned to the 12th Regiment of the 1st Division along with Second Lieutenant Morris who had been in the occupation force in Japan, and had no combat experience. When they reported to Colonel Piak-Sun-Yup, the commander of the 1st Infantry Division, Lewis greeted him in Korean, much to the surprise of the colonel and the lieutenant. The colonel welcomed the advisors and they devised a training plan where Morris would work with the officers and Lewis would train the enlisted men.

Lewis wasted no time organizing his training program. The first morning he rousted out Able Company and broke them into platoons and squads. He showed them how to dress up into formations and do simple military drill. From the ranks he heard one recruit mumble "Ya Man In" or 'barbarian'. Lewis grabbed the offender and, using Cindy Yu's unprintable language, called the young man a "son of a goat." He then turned to the open mouthed recruits and harshly stated in excellent Korean,

"I am Sergeant Lewis Sergeant, of the 101st Airborne Division of the United States Army. I am going to teach you to kill the enemies of your country with guns, knives, rocks or your hands. If you survive this training you will be the toughest company of the toughest division in the Army of the Republic of Korea."

Lewis glared at them for a minute, and then started walking down the ranks. Many of the men straightened up with a look of excitement, while a few drooped with resignation. Lewis drilled them for three hours, and then ran them, by platoons, two miles up a small hill and two miles back. When the exhausted men returned, Lewis told the sergeants to have them count off. Five men were missing, and when they finally straggled in, Lewis sent them to division headquarters as unfit to be combat soldiers. He encouraged competition between the platoons, with the losers digging latrine pits and other onerous tasks. Most of the men in the company had been farmers, and had only the most rudimentary skills, while others from the larger towns and cities were quicker to grasp the basics of modern combat.

William NMI Morris may have been a 'second john' but he wasn't stupid. With ten years experience as a soldier, Lewis could teach him more about combat than he ever learned at officers training school. They worked well together and soon Colonel Paik began to send his fledgling company commanders to meet with Lewis and Morris to study their methods. In Korea, as in most armies, officers take a superior attitude to a noncom and ignore his advice. Lewis quickly debased them of that idea.

"An army is run by its sergeants. Your success as an officer depends on the quality and loyalty of these sergeants. An experienced combat commander knows that one good noncom is worth ten green officers. Promote your noncoms with care and listen to what they have to say."

As the weeks turned into months, Lewis was becoming more and more frustrated by the lack of equipment needed for his regiment. The men had been training with Japanese and M1 rifles. The Japanese rifles had no ammunition and the M1 was too heavy for the smaller Koreans to fire accurately. The men lacked the basic equipment that any army needs to function, such as field packs and good boots. Finally Lewis decided to do something about it, and went to see Joe Chang at the 13th Regiment.

"You know why we can't get any equipment?" he fumed, "It's because that goddamned MacArthur is sending everything to Europe. The ROK Army doesn't have an air force or tanks, artillery and not even carbines." Joe looked at his friend, "Don't blame everything on old 'dugout Doug'. Let's go to Seoul and look up Hausman."

Captain Hausman stood up from his desk and greeted his two visitors.

"Joe, Lewis, what are you guys up to in Seoul?"

"We're going on R&R to Japan and pick up a few supplies from the 8th Army, Joe replied, "and we need a few supply vouchers."

"How many vouchers do you need?"

"About twenty or thirty," Lewis said. The room went silent. Hausman thought. *Damn, these guys are going on a raid. If they get caught it's the stockade*. "What's your plan?" he asked, "If you're thinking big, it's the 15th Quartermaster Company in the 1st Cavalry Division, and you'll need vouchers signed by some infantry commander in the Division to get anything out of the 15th."

"Well Captain," Joe replied, "Lewis and I were thinking about basic stuff that could be carried by a C54, off loaded into covered trucks at Kimpo, then a night trip to the Division."

"You know the supply situation, Captain, we haven't got jack shit to train our men, and those lazy bastards in the 8th have what we need," Lewis continued, "there is going to be war. My men have families in the North, and they tell me that the Commies are getting equipment from China, and even some stuff from the Russians. They're giving them T-34 tanks, Yak fighters, artillery, machineguns and tons of small arms, and God help us if they turn the Mig-15 loose."

Hausman agreed about the coming of war and proceeded to give them some advice that he had learned about the military bureaucracy.

"Remember the old saying he concluded "If you're going to lie, mix in a bit of truth to make it believable." Joe looked at the captain.

"You're a pretty good man for a round eye. If we get caught we'll take the fall."

"D' accord" Lewis agreed.

Captain Hausman was in Army intelligence. He was doing the job of a bird colonel, but without the rank, as he lacked a higher education. More than any other man he created the army of Korea, and he was not going to sit back and let his advisors take the risk alone. He planned to grease the skids.

When 'Captains' Sergeant and Chang arrived at the 15th Quartermaster Company, they were in dress uniform complete with decorations. The CO could not have been more surprised if Moses had appeared, parting the waters. After exchanging salutes he invited them in for coffee. After a few minutes of polite conversation, they got down to business. Lewis, being the best liar, started the ball rolling.

"As you know the Commies have been infiltrating the South for several years. In the past they attacked small villages, but their gangs have grown to a point where they are hitting bigger villages and small towns." Lewis paused then took the plunge.

"Joe and I are part of an advanced team that was organized to train the Korean army to hunt down and wipe out these gangs. It'll take several months for our equipment to get to Korea and we're running out of time. The North is starting to send platoon size units South, and we need to get our men trained and in the field."

"We need to get the necessary equipment from your people and replace it when our stuff gets to Japan. It's top priority on our list." Joe stated.

The CO of the 15th was not accustomed to dealing with plain-spoken Japanese and looked at Lewis.

. "You and Captain Chang are wearing patches of the 101st and the 442nd, both of which have been decommissioned, why is that?" Joe stepped in.

"We are all volunteers from different outfits," he replied,

72

"our unit name is classified, but between us it has the word Ranger in it." Lewis chipped in.

"Joe will be in command as he is the only Medal of Honor winner in the outfit." The CO sprang to his feet and saluted.

"Sorry sir," he stammered, "I've only seen pictures but never a real one."

"Relax Captain," Joe said modestly, "We're all friends here, and besides Lewis never salutes." They adjourned to the officers club for a few drinks, and then a few more drinks. When they finally parted, the CO took the sheaf of vouchers, and promised delivery of the equipment in a week.

The equipment arrived at Kimpo Airfield in one week as was promised, loaded into trucks and transported to the 1st Division Headquarters. Joe and Lewis divvied up the spoils, and the next morning most of the equipment was issued to the excited troops.

With the issue of the new equipment, training intensified. The new M1 Garand carbines were cleaned, broken down and reassembled— again and again and again, until the men could do it in their sleep. Nothing was ever said about the missing 8th Army equipment as Captain Hausman had indeed "greased the skids."

Over the months, the men of the division grew tough and proud of their skill with their weapons. The M1 carbine was perfect for the smaller Koreans. The division had Browning automatic rifles (BARs), .50 caliber machineguns, mortars, bazookas and crates of ammunition. Colonel Paik was a smart, courageous commander, but he was sorely hampered by a lack of tanks and artillery. It was the belief of the U.S. Army brass that tanks would not be effective in the mountainous terrain of Korea. They would be proved to be woefully wrong.

On a Sunday night in June 1950, the North Korean Army, the Inmun Gun, invaded the South. Lewis jumped out of bed as artillery rounds started falling on the regiment. The barrage stopped, and Lewis heard the sound of the bugles that guided the movement of the infantry. A star shell lit up the night, revealing hundreds of troops attacking their position. The North Koreans hit the minefields, and dozens were killed and maimed, but they still kept coming. As it was Sunday, many of the officers and men of the ROK Army, including the newly promoted General Paik, were on leave. Lewis had trained his men for this type of situation, and they grabbed their weapons and started fighting back. Suddenly Lewis heard the clanking sound of tanks, a Russian made T-34 was coming down the road leading to the city of Kaesong. As the tank passed a white range marker, a sergeant pushed a plunger, and blew the T-34 ten feet in the air and dropped it into the deep crater, closing the road. Another tank stopped at the edge of the crater, and the bazooka teams fired, but their 2.36 inch rounds only bounced off the heavy armor. The NKA infantry fell back to regroup and the firing died down. Lewis could now hear heavy firing coming from the 13th and he hoped that Joe was still alive.

Lewis got on the radio and called Paik in Seoul.

"General, we have a problem" he said, "I think we were hit by a full Division." Paik was silent for a moment.

"You don't think that it's just another incursion in force, and do you?"

"No sir there is heavy firing coming from the 13th, and we were plastered by heavy artillery and tanks."

"OK Lewis, I'll grab a jeep and head your way."

"Pick up a few officers too, there's nobody here but us sergeants."

The NKA infantry tried two more assaults the next day, probing the defensive perimeter of the Regiment. The engineers were rapidly repairing the road in spite of the harassing mortar fire. General Paik arrived, and after seeing the situation, decided that he was facing at least two NKA divisions.

Paik was ordered to move his division to the south side of the Han River and defend the capital of Seoul. This would mean the abandonment of Kaesong, and thousands of its residents, but the general had no choice. If he defended the city, he would lose his division.

The division retreated in good order, and tried to destroy supplies and equipment, rather than leaving them for the Inmun Gun. It was a slow retreat, as the roads were clogged with refugees trying to escape the fighting.

The 12th and 13th joined together almost making a

whole regiment. The ROK troops were under constant sniper fire by Communists that mingled with the civilian refugees, using them for cover. The 11th had been overrun, and the men that had not been killed or captured were running for their lives. Russian built Yak fighters bombed the roads, killing more civilians than ROK soldiers. Lewis had seen the same thing in Europe in the last war, the killing of millions of helpless refugees by aircraft.

I guess that pilots must think of people as just targets and not human, he thought. *If they ever saw their work on the ground, the bloody parts of children blown into chunks of meat, they would probably go crazy. Those Yak pilots are Korean, and those refugees are Korean. They are killing their own relatives.*

SERGEANT GOAT / 1950-1953

15

"What did you say, Wonsa?" said Staff Sergeant Kim-Tong-in. He had called Lewis Sergeant Major, and Lewis called him Sergeant Goat, ever since Lewis had slapped him down as a recruit. The kid had been a real wiseass, but he was tough and smart, and willing to learn. He was a natural leader, and Lewis had promoted him to the ranking sergeant in the regiment.

"Just thinking out loud Goat. Civil war is the worst kind of war. "Is your family in Kaesong going to be okay?"

"I hope so Wonsa. My people have a great deal of experience at being conquered. We were a Province of China for hundreds of years. Then came the Mongols, then the Japanese pigs, and now the Communists. But we will survive."

Lewis had developed a real fondness for his young sergeant. The Goat had invited him to Kaesong to meet his family, and Lewis was astonished at the huge tiger pelt that hung on one wall and part of another.

"It's a Siberian tiger," said Kim "My Grandfather killed it with a stick spear as it was tearing a hole in the roof." The little old man, Kim's grandfather, smiled, and explained.

"When the Japanese occupied our Country in 1910, they took our guns, so I made a spear to defend the family. The tiger was old and slow; if it had been a young leopard, it would have killed us all." Lewis thought that the little man could not lift the heavy spear that was hanging on the wall, let alone kill that huge tiger.

"I was young and strong in those days," said the grandfather, reading his thoughts.

As they approached the Han River bridges that led into Seoul, Lewis tried to remember where the ROK army headquarters was located. He saw Joe Chang talking to General Paik, and walked over.

"Wonsa," said Paik, "You and Joe get over to KMAG and locate some ammo, and try to locate Lt. Morris."

They took Paik's Jeep weaving through the mass of humanity. Livestock and carts piled high with possessions clogged the road. Reaching the bridge, they parked the jeep and crossed on foot, Lewis clearing the way with Joe in his wake. Lewis heard someone yelling,

"Yo, you guys first Division? Headquarters wants to talk to your commander." The voice on the radio was tense and short.

"Who's this, and where is Paik?"

"He's with his division about two miles from here, what's this all about?" Lewis replied getting irritated.

"Tell Paik that they are going to blow the bridges in about one hour." Lewis was stunned.

"You're crazy. Half the goddamned ROK Army is north of the Han, nobody would be stupid enough to do that!"

"The Minister of Defense would— to save his ass," said the voice, "so get moving soldier, and good luck," *Not tense now,* Lewis thought, *just sad and very angry*. Lewis handed the mike to the white-faced soldier, and he and Joe took off running back across the bridge. On the other side Lewis told a startled Korean MP Captain what was going on and to get people off the bridge.

They drove slowly North against the flood of tired and frightened people trying to reach the safety of Seoul. They were silent, each with his thoughts. When they were a mile from the bridge, an orange light lit up the sky, and an instant later the sound of the blast hit them. The bridge was gone, trapping most of the of the ROK army north of the Han.

The ROK Army, out gunned, with no armor, very little artillery and antiquated weapons left over from World War II, fought with courage and valor. Thousands were killed fighting the heavy Russian tanks with grenades and obsolete bazookas. The KMAG headquarters in Seoul knew of the inadequate weaponry of the ROK army and prepared for the evacuation of the two thousand men, women and children of the American community. They were evacuated to Japan without the loss of a single man.

KMAG clerks had destroyed all of the important

military files except those files of its four thousand Korean employees. When the Communist Inmun Gun captured Seoul, all of these Koreans were executed. The KMAG advisors that were trapped with their ROK units were on their own.

The United Nations had voted to go to the aid of South Korea, and Truman appointed MacArthur Commander of the UN forces. MacArthur immediately mobilized the 8th Army based in Japan, and sent American planes to assist battered ROK army. The propeller driven Yak fighters were no match for the American jets, and were destroyed or driven from the field. But without ground control they did more harm than good, bombing and strafing friend and foe alike.

The 8th Army in Japan was not the same 8th army that had fought at Luzon, the Philippines, Leyte and taken part in dozens of amphibious landings in the Pacific. After four years of peace it had deteriorated into a soft, ill trained police force. Most of the combat veterans had been replaced by civilian enlistees who had no desire to fight for a backward country like Korea. However it was MacArthur's army so the 8th would go to Korea and teach the "gooks" a lesson.

The Inmun Gun had invaded with over sixty thousand troops, and nearly half of them had been fighting with the Communists against the Nationalists in China for years. Their cadre of officers and noncoms were merciless, and the disobedient were shot on the spot. They were kind to the peasants that they needed to feed their army, but executed thousands of teachers, officials and administrators that could be a future threat to Communist rule. Captured ROK officers were usually tortured and shot.

General Paik Sun Yup was trying to bring the remains of his division across the Han. Lewis and the 12th were fighting a rear guard action against the infantry of the Inmun Gun with some success. The tanks had been stopped by a small bridge that the sappers had destroyed. Until it was repaired the 12th could hold off the unsupported infantry until the 13th had crossed the Han.

Paik was busy rounding up anything that would float to get his men across the river, and did not hear the sound of the approaching fighters. When he did he was immediately flattened and shoved behind a rock by Joe Chang. In a hail of bullets the fearless General jumped up and yelled to his men,

"I told you that the Americans were coming." *Yea, and what a big help they are,* Joe thought sourly.

With most of the 13th on the south side of the river, Paik ordered the 12th to break off the action and retreat to the river, covered by the remainder of the 13th. Lewis, was busy picking off officers and noncoms with his "borrowed" Springfield 1903 sniper rifle, and did not hear the order to retreat. When he paused to reload he saw that he was alone. He ran to catch up with the rest of the regiment, and hearing the rumble of tanks, ran faster. He slid down the riverbank and heard Paik and Joe yelling at him to get his ass in gear. They jumped into a small boat, and were almost to the other side of the Han, when the lead tank arrived. Luckily the T-34 could not depress its cannon enough and the round went high. When they reached the far bank, Lewis shot the tank commander for his trouble.

Seoul was in chaos. Over a million people lived in the capitol and they were all trying to leave at the same time. General Paik had collected his men that had been scattered along the river, and called a meeting of his officers and advisors.

"We must continue to retreat until we meet the American forces. Since we cannot contact the American fighters we must travel the way of the Inmun Gun, only in rainy weather in the day, or at night. We will do what we can with what we have to slow down the enemy until the Americans arrive." Lewis had been translating Paik's Korean to Joe. When the General had finished he looked at his advisors and asked if they had anything to add.

"We have to get those damned fighters to stop bombing and strafing us," said Joe, and Lewis asked,

"Does anyone know where we get a short wave radio?" Seeing the blank looks on their faces he said, "A ham radio?" One of the younger officers brightened and said that there were several over at the KMAG Officer Training School. Lewis looked at Paik, who nodded, and the young officer led them through the mob of refugees to the school. They found four working sets and tried sending messages on different wavelengths, speaking three languages, until they finally got a hit.

Joe started talking rapidly in Japanese. In a few minutes, he looked up and smiled.

"What is that shit eating grin supposed to mean, my inscrutable friend?" Lewis asked.

"It means, my redneck buddy, that even a blind squirrel can find an acorn if he's lucky enough, and you were. The man is a civilian worker for the 8th army, and I gave him the bandwidth." In a few minutes a suspicious voice said,

"This is Captain Arnold, who are you?"

"Sergeant Joe Chang, KAMAG advisor to Colonel Paik's 13th Regiment and with me is Sergeant Lewis Sergeant, advisor to the 12th Regiment."

"And how can I help you Sergeant," he asked.

"By telling those assholes in the Air Force to stop bombing and strafing our division. That's how." In a few minutes the captain came back,

"I can understand that, but how can we identify your unit from the enemy?"

"We'll be waving an American Flag and be traveling in the day. The Inmun Gun travels at night, and hides their tanks and troops in daylight."

"Let me get someone with a higher rank, and I'll try to raise KMAG for you."

"Better hurry the bad guys are crossing the Han, and we're in Seoul."

Lewis told the young officer about the conversation, and to report to the general that we need two American flags, one for each Regiment. He handed the officer a stapler and a box of staples.

"We don't have time to find a seamstress." Lewis and Joe were about to leave when a different voice came over the radio.

"This is General Walker, what's your status and destination." Lewis replied, "The 12th about 50 percent, and looking at Joe, and about the same for the 13th. The 11th was overrun and presumed destroyed sir. Our destination is probably Suwon, but that's General Paik's decision, not mine or Joes."

"If we can drop you a radio can you act as a forward observer for the Air Force?"

"Yes sir," Lewis replied. "Over and out," and they ran back to the division. They found the General bending over a long table with two ragged American flags being stapled by two of his aides. He looked up at them and asked,

"Is it red over white or white over red?"

GENERAL PIAK SUN YUP

16

The regiments formed a column of four files and marched towards Suwon, each flying a tattered American flag with General Paik leading the way in a confiscated jeep. It was a clear day and at 0900 a squadron of F-86 Sabre's appeared, heading in their direction. The flag bearers were frantically waving the red, white and blue rags, with the 48 white dots, as the division anxiously waited for the response. The squadron leader wagged his wings, and they flew off looking for better targets. A flight of Yaks appeared and the Sabre's gave chase. When they were a mile from Suwon, a lone Corsair rolled over Paik's Jeep and dropped a small parachute. It contained a radio, two new American flags, and a note from Captain James Hausman. 'I thought you two guys were dead, I should have known better. Good luck.' General Paik tried out the radio,

"We will be at that grove of trees near Suwon tonight waiting for the Inmun Gun." The pilot said,

"Roger D1" and turned south.

Paik put the 12th in the grove of trees near the road and Lewis and the men with the heavy .50s set up near the road so they could fire directly down the file. The men in the grove would hit the flanks and the 13th would stay in reserve in case of a counterattack. Piak figured that the heavy T-34s would be held up crossing the Han, and the infantry would keep pressing ahead on the remains of the ROK Army. They heard the infantry coming at a fast pace, not wanting to be caught in daylight by the fighters. When they were within fifty feet, the .50 teams opened up, shooting down the road into the files, the heavy slugs ripping through two or three men at a time. When they tried to scatter, the 12th cut them to pieces. The men of the Inmun Gun did not regroup to counterattack, they just turned and ran. Sergeant Kim-Tong-ni looked at the dead, dying and wounded men and spat in the dirt.

"Revenge is sweet," he said. The men of the 12th stripped the soldiers of their grenades and food, and killed any of the wounded that had loot on them. When Sergeant Kim saw a dead soldier with a cape cut from a tiger pelt, he knew his family was dead.

Paik called Lewis and Joe, and handed them a list.

"We're running out of food and ammo. Talk to that pilot and see if we can get an airdrop near Osan." He handed the radio to Joe.

"I can speak better English than the Jap." Joe shot back, "Me no Jap, me Amelican."

Paik shook his head and walked away, shouting to his aides to get organized for the march.

When the Corsair passed overhead the pilot had seen the bodies along the road.

"Nice work guys, what can we do for you today?"

"Can you organize an air drop near Osan? We're running out of food and ammo, need a list?"

"Nope, we know what kind of equipment you have." Joe winked at Lewis. "Good. Be sure to drop plenty of anti-tank mines and a few cases of grenades." The pilot was silent for a minute. Finally he came back.

"Can do buddy."

"Don't bullshit a bullshitter, 'buddy', there ain't an anti-tank mine in Korea, and I doubt if there are any grenades."

"Sorry guys, but I'll see what I can do," the pilot said sheepishly.

The march to Osan was short for a division that could go twenty-five miles at a fast pace. They reached the town at noon. The sky was covered by low clouds and after trying to reach the Corsair, the General decided to head for Ch'onan. There would be no air drop today, and the Inmun Gun would also be on the march.

Lewis was walking a few yards behind Paik, when he saw something that did not look right.

"Sir we should hold here for a minute."

Paik trusted the combat experience of his two advisors, and told the men to grab five. Lewis peered through the sniper scope, and saw a roadblock about a mile distant. He told Paik what he had seen, and asked permission to check it out. Paik nodded, and Lewis jogged ahead a half mile. He had dismounted the scope, and saw clearly an American style helmet behind the barricade. He walked to within a hundred yards, and yelled,

"What outfit?"

"34th what's yours." came the reply.

"1st Division ROK Army," Lewis said, and walked forward, to shake hands with a young captain.

"We heard your outfit was out there, and to look out for you," the captain said. Lewis gave Paik the go ahead signal and the division started moving. A major came up and asked if the NKA was coming.

"Probably less than a day behind us, sir. If you don't have any anti-tank mines you'd better get the hell out." "We have 2.36 bazookas sergeant."

"They just bounce off sir," Lewis interrupted, turned around and walked towards his commander. He briefed Paik, and fell back to the 12th which was bringing up the rear. When the Paik saw the commanding general of the 34th waiting for him, he saluted. They talked for ten minutes while the division marched by, then shook the general's hand and fell in when the 12th arrived.

"Poor bastards," he said sadly. "The general has orders to hold at all costs, and he knows he can't."

At Ch' Onan Paik decided to head for Chonui, a few miles south while there was still enough daylight. Past Chonui they saw another roadblock, manned by the 21st

Infantry. General Paik-Sum-yup decided they had run far enough. He asked the CO of the 21st if he could deploy on the right flank, as the Inmun Gun would attack the center with their tanks and sweep around the flanks with infantry. The CO gave them some ammo as Paik's division was nearly out, and they dug in. At midnight the sound of heavy fire came from the direction of the 34th, and the division held out for almost two days. The rumble of tanks signaled to the troops at Chonui that it was their turn next. Heavy artillery pounded the 21st and 1st and T-34s raked the ridge with machine gun and cannon fire. The 21st artillery countered and two tanks were destroyed. The bugles blew and the Inmun Gun charged the ridge and was met by withering fire from Paik's 1st division and two companies of the 21st. The noncoms fired their weapons; but most of the men hunkered down in their holes. The enemy retreated, regrouped and charged again. One company held and the other was overrun. Paik's 1st counterattacked with the remaining company of the 21st and retook the ridge. They found men with their hands tied behind their backs and shot in the head. A sergeant from the 21st reached into a hole to pull the dog tags from a dead soldier and found a live one underneath. They pulled the man out of the foxhole. He could not walk or speak, and his eyes were like glass.

"Sarge, you should get him covered up, looks like he's in shock," Lewis said. "Tough" said the sergeant, "his buddies M1 is empty—his is full."

That night the enemy infantry climbed the ridge, silent

as fog. They hit tripwires, and the Russian-made grenades blasted huge holes in their ranks, while the guns from the ridge killed most of the rest. They held their position for two days, but when an artillery spotter plane reported that sixteen tanks and at least two enemy divisions were headed their way it was time to get out. They had held, but they paid the price. General Paik's 1st division consisted of one under strength regiment, if the 12th and 13th were combined.

After the angry officers and noncoms of the 21st Division had rounded up most of the 'Bug Outs,' they were only forty percent effective. Lewis heard one disgusted sergeant say, "You ran away you little prick, and the 'gooks' stayed and fought."

The ROK army had lost its best combat divisions north of the Han when the bridges were blown. But the dying divisions had taken thousands of experienced combat solders of the Inmun Gun with them. The further south the NKA went the weaker they got. They could arm themselves with abandoned American equipment, get food from the peasants, and even get volunteers to fill their ranks, but they could not replace their armor or their hard core veterans. After tasting the brutality of Communism, many of these 'volunteers' slipped away, or surrendered.

In the south the ROK army divisions were slowly built up with volunteers, and veterans that had escaped from the devastated divisions in the north. The Minister of Defense, who had ordered the destruction of the Han River bridges, was executed.

Paik's 1st and the 21st formed a defensive line north of Chochi won, but could not hold against the armor and artillery of the Inmun Gun. They retreated to Taejon and joined the battered 34th to defend the city.

The North Koreans had infiltrated the city disguised in American uniforms, and were sniping at the rear of the defense. Lewis and the Goat were killing every soldier with a baggy uniform. They were surprised by seeing General Dean with a ROK bazooka man crouched in the next building, aiming at a T-34. The shell hit the tank and destroyed it with two more rounds. "I wish we had some of those," said the Goat wishfully. They had held up the Inmun Gun for three days, and when they retreated, they had to fight their way out through the North Korean Army to get to Pusan. The 1st ROK and the 21st, held a roadblock for a day, and had to withdraw to keep from being surrounded, while tanks from the 1st Cavalry Division helped the 34th escape. General Walker had sent in the 24th and 1st Cavalry Divisions towards Taejon to help defend the city, but they met the Immun Gun and retreated over ninety miles to Pusan. During the retreat, Paik's emaciated division fought more like guerillas than a division. The 21st had half the men they had when they first encountered the North Koreans, but that half had become tough and hardened veterans, and fought with skill and courage. The 1st Cavalry M24 light tanks were no match against the heavy T-34 and were destroyed when they encountered them. Without help from the Air Force, they would have never made it back to Pusan.

While General Paik's 1st division was placed on the perimeter of the line protecting Pusan, Lewis and Joe were called to KMAG headquarters. General Walker wanted a briefing on the skills of the 1st Division and why it was so effective against the North Korean Army. Lewis looked at Joe, and nodded, *give him both barrels*, Joe winked back. They had been together so long they had an almost telepathic sense of communication.

"First" Joe said, "They had a superb leader in General Paik, and his cadre of officers. They could re-arm themselves from the dead enemy soldiers, and abandoned supplies from fleeing Americans." Lewis said.

"We knew the tactics of the Immun Gun, and when to fight and when to run. When we had good terrain, we fought, and killed ten of them for one of us." They talked for an hour why the ROK Army should have good weapons, like artillery, the 3 inch bazookas and 60 mm mortars. They talked of the battles they had fought and what they had learned, and how Paik had defeated the enemy.

General Walker listened in silence. Finally he said,

"You are KAMAG Advisors, so give me some advice."

"First give every green outfit that comes off the boat a three day briefing, and the way home is to fight or go home in a basket." Joe said,

"And Paik's troops had pride in their colors, and would not leave their wounded behind," Lewis added, "and none of our men were ever captured."

Walker stood up and shook hands with Lewis and saluted Joe, and walked away. "Christ Joe you sure milk that medal."

"Tough shit," said the inscrutable Nisi. They returned to the division. General Paik was alone, having sent his officers out to find young Koran's that wanted to fight rather work as laborers for the Americans.

"My friends I have news for you. Since you won't accept a battlefield commission, you both have been given promotions to Sergeant Major. Joe will remain here with the 1st to train our new recruits. He looked at Lewis, and you will be detached from my command to brief newly arrived French Battalion. They are mostly Algerians, and speak French; you do speak French, right?"

"No speakee Flench," Lewis replied.

The Algerians were mostly from the French Army that had fought in the wars for independence in Libya. They had fought against the FLN to keep Algeria French, and 'Algerie Francaise' was their battle cry. They were professional soldiers, and were contemptuous of the North Korean peasant army that they had been sent to fight. Lewis showed the infantry battalion where to bivouac, and gathered the officers and noncoms together for an initial briefing.

As he had expected the officers protested against the presence of the noncoms. Lewis told them that the noncoms would get the same briefing as the officers and he did not want to repeat himself. When the French commander asked him about his combat experience, Lewis told him that he was with the BEF when the Germans beat the French Army and pushed the BEF into the sea at Dunkirk. And was with the 101st when they dropped into France, and fought with the Marques against the Germans. The commander thanked him for the information and asked him to continue.

"It is a peasant army that has fought against the Nationalists, the Japanese, and now the U.S. and ROK armies. They are tough, experienced and not afraid to die." Lewis told them about the tactics used by the Immun Gun and their strengths and weaknesses. When he had finished his briefing the commander asked him if he knew the leader of the Marques in Normandy.

"Marie Vasquez", Lewis said, "the Black Widow." The officers and most of the noncoms knew of her.

"That's one tough lady." the commander remarked, and the briefing ended.

General Paik's 1st Division was filling out with young Koreans eager to fight. Lewis and Joe worked in a frenzy trying to get the men ready. The Inmun Gun was going to hit them hard and they did not have much time.

When the Pusan perimeter was attacked it came from all directions at once. The attack came at night and hit the perimeter between Paik's 1st and the U.S. 25th Division. The two Divisions fell back to protect their flanks, and avoiding the NKA's attempt to attack their rear. It was the same tactic used on all of the ROK Divisions defending the north end of the perimeter. The attack failed. The once powerful Inmun Gun was a shell. Most of its armor had been destroyed and most of the veterans killed. The green men of the infantry that attacked were driven by fanatical officers and noncoms. Attack or be shot in the back was a powerful incentive.

BREAKOUT

17

On September 15th, 1950 the Marines landed at Inchon quickly overcoming the weak resistance of the North Korean Army, and pressed on to Seoul. Since the Americans would never trade real estate for lives most of the capitol was reduced to rubble. The U.N. forces broke out of the Pusan perimeter and pushed the Inmun Gun northward. Their supply lines cut, and attacked from all sides, thousands were captured or disappeared into the mountains to fight as guerrillas. MacArthur's plan was to reunite Korea, and he pressed northward towards the Yalu river, the border between China and Korea.

Korea was and always had been a buffer country between China and Japan. The Chinese were determined that if Korea was to be united it would be under Communism. As the U.N. forces pushed the North Koreans northward, the Chinese sent thousands of men and equipment south across the Yalu River. By November 1950, 180,000

Chinese were waiting for the 8th and ROK armies, and 120,000 were hiding in the mountains around the Chandjin Reservoir. The Chinese commanders realized that the U.N. controlled the skies and maintained superb camouflage discipline. They moved their divisions at night and hid in the rugged mountains and valleys during the day. When the 8th Army reached the Ch'ongh'on River the Chinese attacked.

From the port city of Hungnam on the Sea of Japan, the Marines 5th and 7th Divisions marched towards the Changjin reservoir. The Chinese had massed 100,000 men north of the village of Yudam-ni and in the arctic night they attacked the Marines and the Army X corps with seven infantry Divisions; Two Divisions were at Yudam-ni, three at Hagaru-ri and two at Koto-ri. The Marines held and in the daylight the Chinese were savaged by American aircraft.

During the long retreat from the Changjin reservoir to the port of Hungnam, there were as many casualties from frostbite and dysentery as from battle wounds. The Marines and Army took their dead, wounded and all of their equipment to Hungnam and loaded aboard Navy ships, along with the ROK 1st Corps that had advanced to the Yalu. Last to board were the thousands of Korean refuges from the devastated city of Hungnam.

On the night of November 29th Lewis was leading a recon unit halfway up a ridge a mile ahead of Paik's 1st Division. They ran into at least two Chinese infantry divisions. Sergeant Kim-Tong-ni threw a grenade, and the explosion alerted the 1st that trouble was coming their way. The 1st spread across the valley and met the Chinese with heavy fire from the front and flanks. A star shell lit up the valley reveling thousands of Chinese infantry, bugles blowing and screaming 'Manzai Manzai.' The heavy BARs and .50 caliber machine guns stopped the Chinese, and they fell back to regroup and attack again.

The ROC II Corps losses were extreme, and the American 8th Calvary to the left was overwhelmed and destroyed. As the units on either side of Paik's 1st division melted away, General Paik had to retreat. Lewis and the Goat had to change barrels on the .50 as the first one had been worn out in the fight. They were joined by the remnants of the 8th that had escaped. Of the thousand men of the 8th only 10 officers and 200 men survived. At daylight the Chinese broke off the attack and disappeared into the mountains.

When General Paik heard that the British 29th Gloucester Regiment was ordered to hold their position he could not believe it. He radioed command and told the CO that the regiment faced fifty to sixty thousand Chinese. He was told that a relief column was on the way, and several units tried to reach them, the Filipinos, Belgians, Puerto Ricans and American tanks. They all failed. The Chinese were strafed and bombed by American aircraft, but they kept on attacking the Gloucesters. They held out for three days before they were overrun. Out of more than 600 men of the Gloucestershire Regiment only 32 survived. The Glosters had held up the Chinese divisions for three days, giving the 8th Army time to consolidate, and to dig in. Facing a wall of steel and guns, the Chinese command decided to regroup and fight another day.

With the 1st Division safely dug in, Lewis, Joe and the Goat borrowed a jeep and went looking for beer. An enterprising Korean family had turned their little hooch into a bar and served cold beer from an ice chest. While they were enjoying their Nippon Three Star, a jeep load of officers from the 21st drove up and sat down, all except one very green lieutenant.

"I don't drink with Japs or gooks," he said, and before his fellow officers could move Lewis was out of his chair, grabbed the Lieutenant, and shook him until his teeth rattled.

"Apologize to my friends," he snarled, "Or I'll tear off your fucking head and spit down your neck hole" The officers apologized for the rudeness of the lieutenant and left, the shaken lieutenant muttering about a court marshal.

"Hell Lewis you call me a Jap. all the time," Joe said. Lewis grinned at him.

"Yup but you're my Jap." The Goat was mystified. He hadn't understood a word.

The next day the commander of the 21st called General Paik. They spoke for a few minutes then the CO of the 21st said,

"You mean Joe Chang? Thank you General, I'll take care of It."

That afternoon the sergeant major of the 21st called Lewis.

"What the hell happened? I've never seen the old man so pissed off.

"I don't know, I just got a little carried away, *God help me for shaking up the little prick, could be stockade city.* Don't know Top, what happened on your end?"

"That shavetail went in to see the general, and then the general called Paik. The old man shut the door, and he don't do that unless he's really going to ream some ass.

"What happened."

"I filled out a transfer form and when I got to the spot where it says destination I asked him "to where" and he told me to leave it blank. Today the kid's gone."

"Too bad Top. Tough to loose such a promising young officer." And they both laughed.

During the next two weeks the Chinese and North Koreans built up their forces with men and weapons. Despite harassment from the air, the buildup went rapidly. The air power of the U.N. was not effective against a hidden enemy in the rugged mountains of Korea.

While the Chinese were adding manpower to their armies, the U.N. was digging deeper. On May 16 1951 140,000 Chinese and 35,000 North Koreans were moving south. The Chinese sang as they marched, and the mountains rang with the sound. The sky was overcast and the U.N. aircraft grounded and impotent. The Chinese and North Korean armies hit the ROC army, which held, then finally had to retreat or be annihilated. They ran into two U.N. infantry divisions and the 72nd Tank Battalion, and were stopped by fire and steel.

Badly hurt they tried punching through the 2nd and 38th Infantry Divisions. C Company of the 38th was overrun but the gap was plugged by the French Battalion. They then attacked Hill 255, which was heavily fortified by the 3rd Battalion 38th Division. The Chinese took the hill then were thrown off with a counter attack by the 3rd. By the 21st of May, under the hammering of the U.N. air, artillery and armor the Chinese were no longer an effective fighting force. The 8th Army counterattacked and continued to hold the initiative. The 8th Army continued pursuit North above the 38th parallel then it was halted, not by arms but by the United Nation truce talks.

The Chinese, emboldened by the apparent weakness of the United Nations at the truce talks, continued mass attacks against the 8th Army. These attacks were easily repulsed, with heavy losses by the Chinese and North Korean armies. When the U.N. was willing to accept a cease fire and withdraw to the 38th Parallel, the South Koreans were enraged. They had suffered the destruction of their towns and cities; they had lost one million three hundred thousand men, women and children. Millions were homeless, and thousands of orphaned children, and widowed women were starving in the rubble. All of this pain and suffering to return to the status quo. They could not even plead their case; they had no seat at the Truce Talks as a ward of the U.N.

HILL 255 / 1953

18

Joe and Lewis were called to division headquarters by General Paik.

"Joe you and Lewis have enough points to return to the States." They looked at the general waiting for the other shoe to drop. Finally, Joe said,

"I've had enough of this war, its time to go home."

"How about you Lewis?" Lewis was looking at Joe and didn't seem to hear his commander.

"You getting out Joe?"

"The family is having trouble getting their farm back. Some clown from 'Frisco says he owns it"

"Need some help?"

"Thanks Lewis, but I can handle it. You're a lifer. Better stick around and keep the general out of trouble."

"After all of my kindness, my generosity you say that?" Paik tried to look offended but cracked when his two sergeants started laughing. They reminised for a while as men do when they had shared the fire and blood of war. Then Lewis said,

"General, with your permission I'd like to see Joe off."

"No problem Lewis, the 7th needs an interpreter to question some NKA soldiers. You can catch up with Joe in Japan."

Lewis agreed, and as they were leaving Paik said,

"And by the way I am giving your friend Kim-Tong-ni a battlefield commission, so don't forget to salute him." Joe and Lewis saluted the bewildered Goat, and told him of his promotion. The new lieutenant was so happy he offered to go with Lewis to the 7th Division and help with the prisoners. They reported to division headquarters, and were told that the North Koreans were being held by Easy Company on Hill 255.

They arrived at Easy Company and were questioning the prisoners when they heard the sound of gunfire. The Chinese had overrun the 1st Platoon and were taking over their bunkers. Grabbing two boxes of ammo and a .50 caliber machinegun, Lewis and the Goat moved towards the gunfire. Holding the heavy weapon at waist level, Lewis shot two Chinese, but a third shot the Goat.

As he fell Kim-Tong-ni looked at Lewis, and shook his head as if to apologize, and with blood gushing from his mouth he died. Lewis looked at his friend then pried the dead fingers from the boxes of ammo. Slinging two bandoleers over his shoulders, he walked down the line of bunkers, killing every Chinese in sight. Mortar fire started raining down on the hill but he didn't seem to notice. When a chunk of shrapnel ripped out his eye, he simply shook off the gore and continued killing.

A lieutenant and two sergeants followed Lewis with Tommy guns and a case of grenades, killing Chinese hiding in the bunkers. When two men tried to surrender, Lewis blew their heads off with a burst from the .50. As the mortar fire intensified, the lieutenant yelled at Lewis to get under cover, but he did not seem to hear, and went on killing Chinese. He was shot twice in the legs and knocked down by a burst of shrapnel. He got up, dripping blood and gore arrived at the tip of the hill. A fresh company of Chinese was approaching from the Northwest, while two companies from the 7th were attacking from the south. Seeing the undefended ridge and only one lone solder, the Chinese charged.

Lewis was chopping down Chinese like wheat, when the lieutenant and the sergeants joined him with Tommy guns and grenades. Seven Chinese charged up the remaining few yards to the crest, and one of the sergeants was killed. Lewis had run out of ammo and, using the .50 like a club, bashed in the head of one soldier. But a big Chinese corporal rammed a bayonet into his stomach, shot it free, and hit Lewis in the head with a butt stroke. The lieutenant stitched the corporal as he was bending over Lewis's body, and the sergeant killed the rest.

A tired medic looked down at the bloody body. He didn't think that the Korean sergeant was alive but he checked for a pulse, found a faint beat and called in a MASH helicopter. The Easy Company lieutenant wiped the blood off of the shoulder patch of a ROK army 1st Division soldier and identified Sergeant Major Lewis Sergeant. The men of the 7th packed up their gear and left the hill for the Communists. Since it was on the north side of the 38th parallel it was not worth defending as it would belong to North Korea anyway. The lieutenant shook his head in disgust. *All that blood for one piece of worthless real estate. I hope the Chinks pick a more fitting name than Pork Chop, Chop Suey would be better.*

On the 16th of April 1953 the Korean War ended for Sergeant Major Lewis Sergeant. He was transported to a MASH field hospital where the doctors managed to pump in enough blood to keep him alive, sewed up his wounds and sent him to the 8th Army hospital in Japan. His skull was fractured and the heel of the rifle stock had also put in a dent that required a steel plate. The stomach wound was the worst. When the corporal had fired the weapon to free the bayonet it blew in dirt, clothing and other debris into the wound. The other wounds could wait. If he survived they could take care of them one at a time.

Doctor Roberts kept him sedated as he feared that without anesthetics Lewis would die of shock from the trauma. One day the nurse was about to give him a maintenance dose when she saw a bright green eye looking at her. It croaked something and she called Dr. Roberts. He looked at Lewis who glared at him and said "Goat." When the nurse held up the syringe, and looked at the doctor, Lewis gave a sharp grunt. Roberts told the nurse not to give him any anesthetics unless he asked for them. All Lewis would ask for was APCs or aspirin. When an 8th army

general told him that he was going to get his nations highest award he looked at the man with the stars and said, What for? He remembered looking at the Goat and then the nurse and nothing in between. But he did remember one word the man said and that word was Discharge.

One day Dr Roberts came in and was talking to the head nurse. She called him Colonel, and through the red mist of pain, Lewis saw a chink in the doctors medical armor. The Colonel was the best of the best of army trauma surgeons. He was renown for his skill and unflappable demeanor, until he met the sergeant major. As the doctor and nurse were walking over to his bed Lewis called out,

"Hey Bobby, can you fix this head pain?" Colonel Roberts stiffened.

"We can always amputate," he said and walked away.

"Thanks Bobby" Lewis called out, ignoring the angry expression of the nurse.

This was the opening salvo of what was to be known as "The Bob and Goliath War." Dr. Roberts was the only one that could pronounce Lewis 'fit for duty' and he saw it as his professional duty not to do it. The patient had only one eye, a bullet near his spine that could not be removed, a head pain that may never stop, and a real bad attitude.

Only a fool would pronounce the man 'fit for duty' and the doctor was no fool.

Joe had driven to the MASH field hospital, but was unable to see his friend. When Lewis was moved to Japan Joe was waiting. He waited for a week, then went back to help his family in the states. He convinced the interloper that he had 'leased' the property from the Chang family for the duration of their imprisonment. He spent a few days with his family then returned to Japan.

Lewis's battle strategy was a simple frontal attack, envelope the enemy and force a surrender. He admired the doctor and respected his professionalism. He had also admired and respected the professional soldiers that he had killed. When Joe walked into the ward, Lewis was trying to stand up with the help of an orderly and a young nurse. Joe was shocked at the sight of his almost indestructible friend, but he relaxed when he looked into that fierce green eye.

"You look like shit."

"What do you expect with a quack like that one?" he said, nodding towards Colonel Roberts who was bending over the bed of another patient.

"Yo, Bobby come over and meet my friend Joe"

Roberts was seething but outwardly was the cool professional.

"Pleased to meet you sergeant … ah Chang," he said looking at Joes name tag. "But visiting hours start at 1300 and you'll have to leave."

"Bobby you forgot to salute" Colonel Roberts saw the

ribbon, mentally damned both Joe and Lewis to hell, and saluted. Joe returned the salute, nodded to the doctor and started talking to Lewis.

"Paik buried him with full military honors."

"I heard that Joe. You get the family squared away?"

Colonel Roberts turned and walked away from the pain of the two sergeants. Unfit for duty… it would be kinder to shoot him.

Lewis spent the remainder of 1953 in the hospital, and was fitted with a glass eye. In January of 1954, he was flown to Washington to receive the decoration by the new President Eisenhower. He was 36 years old.

AFRICA / 1954 to 1961

19

Tiger Tiger Burning Bright
In The Forests Of The Night
What Immortal Hand Or Eye
Could Frame Thy Fearful Symmetry

William Blake

After the stalemate in Korea, the blockade of Berlin and other excursions by the Communists, the American people knew that they were in a war. A war of a different kind, called the Cold War, but still a war.

Pop was still called "Wonsa" by the officers and noncoms, and that name was picked up by the draftees and volunteers that he trained at Breckinridge. The sergeant major trained both officers and men. He advised the officers and hammered the lower ranks. He wanted knowledgeable leaders that would not get men killed without a good reason. Most of the officers listened to his advice with attention and respect. A few that

111

did not like being instructed by a noncom, complained to the commanding officer. After listening to their complaints, he sent them to supply school. He didn't want whiners in the infantry. Fresh off the bus, the new recruits were formed into rank and file, by the drill instructors. The first sergeant marched to the front of the ranks and told them that the sergeant major will address them. Pop stepped to the front and gave his usual peroration;

'"You men are citizens of the United States of America, the greatest country in the world. You are not soldiers. In eight weeks you will swear to defend the Constitution of the United States, and then you will be soldiers. In those eight weeks you will learn the basic fighting skills of the infantry. Some of you will be sent to supply school or trained as cooks or other non-combat jobs. But remember an army without logistical support, food, ammo and a hundred other things is not an army—just a mob in uniform. Just because you are a mechanic or clerk doesn't mean you are safe in the rear. An artillery shell is indifferent as to what it kills—cook or general. In combat you are not fighting for mom and country, you fight for your friends and foxhole buddy. You kill the enemies of your country, and some of you will die. That's what a soldier gets paid to do." The men were then dismissed to the tender mercies of the noncoms.

After two years of training men to be soldiers, Lewis felt he needed a break. So he talked to the CO about taking some leave time. The CO told him that anyone with the "Medal" could take all the leave he wanted. The CO was a veteran of the Korean War, and felt that his sergeant major was one of the best at turning civilians into soldiers. But the word from upstairs was to, ease off, as there had been too many complaints. Lewis didn't know he had become an anachronism, somewhat famous in military circles, but still an anachronism. So Lewis took his leave, unaware of his commander's relief. He was gone for three years.

My dad had always liked animals. No matter what size or species, wild or tame, he just liked animals. He loved women and his family and friends but he never told them that they were loved. He lived in a time where the word love was not said aloud by men. It was understood but never spoken. Pop had never seen the animal he liked best in the wild, the Bengal Tiger. He had seen them in carnivals, a circus and zoos, but never in their natural surroundings. He had seen them in tiny cages with no room to roam, sleeping in their own feces, and fed rotten food. So he decided to get his own tiger.

In 1955 the way wild animals were displayed had changed little since Roman times. People looked at animals in cages and the animals looked back at the people. The animals may have been psychotic but the people were entertained. An orangutan at the Bronx zoo was famous for luring people near by crooking his finger, and when they were within range he would throw his shit at them. Lewis wanted his own tiger, and in his quest for the perfect animal he would rely on this friends, and the military network that spanned the globe. The man to start with was his friend Vinnie in New York.

Vinnie had returned to New York with some of Goring's hoard and, applying the skills that he had learned in combat and on the black market, had become a rich man.

"Christ on a crutch," he said when he saw Lewis, "You look like Cyclops with a hangover." He worked a network of men who "borrowed" things, and sometimes broke a few bones to keep in practice. He had perfected his talent for finding anything, for anyone, for any purpose.

They sat in Vinnie's bar. Over drinks and dinner Lewis filled him in on Korea. They joked about the old times in France and Germany and Vinnie's ability to keep their outfit well supplied. They were very comfortable with each other. Vinnie told Lewis about New York being "Ground Zero" and about the air raid drills to get into the subway or under the table. "We have at least twenty minutes," he bragged.

Lewis told him that it would be the best thing for the country if New York got hit by a nuke. He was joking, but like most westerners he did not care for the rude, sometimes arrogant New Yorkers. Vinnie was offended, and Lewis comforted him with the lie that New York had a good plan and that most of them would survive. Vinnie perked up,

"Hell Lewis, with all these nukes around we don't need an army, work for me and start out as a collector. With your size and that eye the deadbeats would stuff the take and twice the vig in your bag."

Lewis didn't understand a word he said, but when he

figured it out, Vinnie saw the look in the green eye and quickly changed tack.

"But hell Lewis, you wouldn't fit in here, you'd bust up some made guy and get shot in the back." Lewis thanked him for the offer and asked him if he could still get anything for anyone.

"You name it, and I'll get it." Lewis explained what he wanted and Vinnie wrote it down.

"A Bengal tiger male cub, six to eight weeks old and off the mother's tit. The mother has to be bred from a male from another zoo—I don't want a cross eyed reject first cousin cub and I don't want one that's following his mother. I want him to follow me." They went to Vinnie's flat above the bar and he showed Lewis his "bunk" complete with bathroom, kitchen and king size bed.

"I'll send you up a woman. This is going to take some time," he said and left.

When the woman arrived Lewis was making lunch and offered her a plate. She thanked him and sat down to eat. She charged two hundred dollars an hour, and had been paid for the night, so feed or fuck it was all the same. He asked her about New York and got the stock answers about the tallest building, Central Park and so on. Lewis asked her about the famous New York library. She faltered a bit, as she had no idea where it was, but gamely said it was real big and full of books. When she glanced at her watch, Lewis figured that it was time for business and led her into the bedroom, and hung their clothes neatly in the closet.

Lewis liked variety and she was very experienced so they bounced around on the big bed. Every time she thought he was finished, he started up again, until she finally called a halt. After dinner Lewis changed the sheets and they went to bed. The woman rolled over and went to sleep and Lewis read one of Vinnies few books, about venereal disease. When she woke up the next morning, they had a 'Dawn Buster' before she left.

Vinnies crew looked in every zoo in the big cities of several states. They finally found a female with three four week old cubs, and she had mated with a tiger from another zoo. The zoo administrator agreed to sell the male cub after it had been weaned, so Lewis went to Chicago to check out the mother and cub. The mother was a big healthy Bengal tigress and the cub was fat and active. He drove upstate to see the male at the other zoo. He was a huge sleek Bengal that paced to the limits of his cage, indifferent to the people outside. He stopped when he saw Lewis and looked into his eye. Lewis saw, in those fierce Tiger eyes, a yearning so strong that he had to turn away.

He went back to Chicago and spent the next four weeks watching and listening to the mother and her cubs. She "talked" to the cubs with chuffs, snorts and other, almost inaudible sounds, with an occasional cuff on the ear. In a week Lewis made a few tiger sounds and the male cub waddled over to the bars and peered at him. The mother did not like the cub near the bars, and bounded over, grabbed the cub by the nap of the neck and dropped him in with his sisters. At the end of three weeks Lewis walked into the cage, picked up the cub, looked at the mother, and walked out. *This little bugger isn't going into a cage like his father, he's going to Africa.*

Lewis hitched a ride in a military DC-3 that was going to New York. When he arrived at Vinnie's bar, he went upstairs to settle up. Figuring that he owed Vinnie several thousand dollars, and was surprised when he said,

"You don't owe me a damned thing." They argued a few minutes, then Lewis pulled out a handful of trinkets from his carryall and put them on the table.

"They're from the fat bastards hoard. Ma didn't like the ring but she loved the cross and wears it to church." Vinnie looked at the small pile of trinkets and told Lewis that the diamond in the ring was worth more than his bar and ten like it. "Take it, pay your men, and keep the rest for yourself."

"I'll keep half and send you the rest Sarge."

"Kiss my ass Corporal," Then they went to play with the cub.

BENGAL

20

The Bengal tiger is the second largest cat species in the world, and a full grown male can weigh over seven hundred pounds. A big tiger has three-inch fangs, and can attack at speeds of over forty miles an hour. They can range over twenty miles in a night searching for prey. The males are mostly solitary except when breeding. The female makes a chuffing, low groaning-growling sound when in heat. Tigers will eat any kind of meat, fish, fowl or human. Some older, slower tigers in India became infamous man-eaters, and had eaten hundreds of people before being shot. Pop had read many books about tigers, written mostly by the men who had shot them. He had no illusions about the cub. He wanted a friend, preferably one that wouldn't eat him.

There were no military flights from the States to Africa, and Lewis was stumped until he thought of going by ship. He did not like boats as they floated on water, but he had no other choice. Most of the shipping to Africa from France, so he called Marie and asked her if she knew what was available. She said she would make inquires and for him to come to Paris. He hopped a C-123 Provider going to France, and Marie met him at the airport. They went to her apartment and swapped war stories. He asked her about her love life.

"So so," she said wagging her fingers. "Most of them are dumb and boring and the smart ones don't stick around."

"Still working for the OSS or CIA as they call it now?" Lewis asked, and was surprised when she said yes. She was giving him her CIA appraisal look, when the cub, who had been stalking her shoe, pounced for the kill.

"If that damned cat shits on my rug he's history," she said peevishly. Lewis was beginning to feel a bit wary, but she didn't have that look in her eyes before she killed something, so he relaxed.

"Do you know anything about the Congo?" she asked. Lewis had planed to go to Niger and see the fantastic Mastiffs of the Air Mountains, but he was also interested in the jungles of the Congo. When she saw his interest, she said she could get him to the Congo free, if he would do a little favor for the Company. He raised a quizzical eyebrow. A favor from the Company could get you killed. Marie told him the Details;

"A man named Joseph Vedts went to France in '38 as a young man to fight with the Belgians against the Nazis. He returned to the Congo in '46 an old man. He had been captured in the blitzkrieg and used as slave labor in a Nazi factory. He is a Belgian and was in the Congo working for De

Beers as a geologist. He hates De Beers and the Germans equally. He has something for me and I want you to get it. I'll contact him and he will find you. There are not too many-one eyed Yanks with a tiger in a place where there are no tigers. The *General Mangin* sails from Marseilles for Point Norie in four days." She knew Lewis would go so she did not bother to ask.

He stayed in her apartment four days and trained the cub, feeding him goat's milk and small pieces of meat. He would hide a fish or dead mouse, and the cub would stalk and "kill" the prey. Lewis would "talk" to it, but would not touch the cub except for an occasional cuff. He followed Lewis around the apartment and slowly, with great patience Lewis taught him to kill.

Marie drove him to Marseilles. Before they boarded, he asked her if the CIA knew that they had a 'Dick Tracy' in their ranks. She smiled. "Any friend of Bill's is a friend of theirs." She handed him a thick envelope, climbed in her car and drove away.

The *General Mangin* was a small cruise ship with room for three hundred passengers. Lewis had a first class cabin for himself and his cat. During the long voyage he read the history of the Congo and Niger, and walked his cat around the deck. If a passenger wanted to pet the cub, Lewis would say he bites, and that usually ended the matter. One day he remembered the envelope Marie handed him. Opening it, he found $10,000 and an unsigned note saying 'your share.'

There were actually two Congos and the one the ship

was heading for was leaning towards Communism. This was called the Republic of the Congo. The other was the Democratic Republic of the Congo which was a Parliamentary Democracy. Lewis wasn't very happy about the Communist part but found it interesting that both countries spoke French, and were friendly to France. *Africa is full of intrigue, he* thought, *like "Days of our Lives"—with blood.* He read Marie's notes about de Beers, and figured out why Joseph hated them so much. He finished the book and went to sleep.

JOSEPH VEDTS

21

When the ship reached Point Norie, Joseph Vedts was waiting for him on the dock. Lewis was trying to avoid him, but was immediately surrounded by a mob of laughing, joking Congolese. One of them finally asked him in French if it was a baby lion. Lewis answered that it was a baby tiger and thinks that I am his mother. They howled at the thought of this big, ugly one eyed man being a mother, and Lewis laughed with them.

"I'll bring him back in a year and he'll eat one of you for lunch," he said. They all pointed at a little fat man,

"Him, him," they shouted, and rolled on the ground as the little man scurried away.

So much for being inconspicuous, Lewis thought as he shook hands with Joseph. They went through Customs where an official eyed Lewis's American passport. He opened it, closed it, and said with a broad smile. "Welcome to our country." and Lewis was in the People's Republic of the Congo. The hundred dollar bill was missing from the passport, but no harm no foul.

Joseph Vedts was a small skinny man with bad teeth. His eyes darted around suspiciously as they walked to his house. *He's a rotten spy*, Lewis thought, *but maybe he has to be a bit paranoid if half of what I read about de Beers is true*. On the small veranda they sat on rocking chairs that operated the long overhead sweeps that kept the flies away. They sat in silence until Lewis finally remarked that Joseph had a fine comfortable house. Joseph beamed.

"I built it myself before the war," he said and gave Lewis a tour. It was a beautiful house, hand crafted with the lustrous dark wood from the jungle.

Back on the veranda Joseph hesitantly asked Lewis if he would like to use the spare bedroom.

"But the hotel is nice," he added hastily.

"If the cub doesn't bother you I would very much like to." Lewis replied. They talked until midnight, the war being common ground. They both agreed that every Gestapo agent and SS bastard should have been hung at Nuremberg. Joseph asked him what he was going to name the cub. Lewis said that he was going to name him Herman since Goering had paid for him. When Lewis explained, the little man convulsed with laughter. Lewis smiled at the reaction to the small joke. Apparently Joseph had little to laugh about in his life. They went to bed and just before Lewis fell asleep he put his pistol under his pillow. Customs hadn't opened his carryall and found the Walther

P-38. The hundred dollar bill was a good investment.

Joseph was a geologist and had graduated from a good school in Belgium.

"de Beers hired me because I was a Belgian and could speak French. I was more of a prospector for kimberlitic deposits than a geologist. The company had found diamonds in the Congo and they wanted me to find more." He had almost choked on the word diamond, and was stammering, so Lewis changed the subject.

"Joseph, see those birds in that tree? Stand still and I'll show you something." He gave a few clicks and whistles and the birds flew down and around their heads. Joseph climbed out of his dark mood and said,

"Lewis, don't do that trick around the blacks. Most of them are Christians, but underneath many of them still believe in the old gods and spirits."

The next day they packed for a hike in the bush. While Joseph was fixing sandwiches, Lewis pulled out the P-38 and the shoulder holster and slipped it on. He put on a muslin sling to carry the cub, when Joseph walked in and saw the pistol. "Is that for me Lewis?" he asked in a calm voice. Lewis was perplexed, and then it dawned on him that he thought Lewis was going to kill him. He was stunned, and it showed. Joseph smiled.

"I'm a crazy old man Lewis. I trust Marie and I trust you and I'm very sorry for having offended you." They hiked several miles to a little patch of trees that had not been cut down for crops or grass and sat down.

"Let me tell you about the business of diamonds," and began his long bitter story.

"In the eighteen seventies a man found an 83 carat diamond in Kimberly, South Africa and started the great African diamond rush. A man named Cecil Rhodes sold pumps to the miners, and bought mining claims with the profits. By 1890 he owned almost all the claims in South Africa. Rhodes negotiated with a London company to fix the price of diamonds. When the demand was up they made millions and when demand was down they made less money but the price never changed. They either stopped mining operations, or stockpiled the diamonds.

To keep his monopoly, he obtained backing from Alfred Beit and Rothschild and Sons and bought claims all over Africa. In 1927 the "Anglo American PLC," controlled by Oppenheimer and J.P. Morgan took control. In 1935 de Beers obtained a ninety-eight- year lease on all the diamond fields in South Africa. The company is named de Beers but Oppenheimer is in control.

Gem quality diamonds are a luxury but industrial diamonds are a necessity. They have a thousand uses, drilling, machining high tolerance parts or making gyroscopes for submarines. Eighty percent of these diamonds were in the hands of de Beers. When the RAF needed fighter planes from America, the Americans could not make them fast enough because of the shortage of diamonds. Who controlled the supply? de Beers. Hitler had plenty of diamonds, paid for with the gold from a million Jewish mouths. The

OSS knew, but they had no proof." Joseph paused, his eyes misting over as he recalled the horrors of the past.

"By slowing down war production in the west and supplying the Axis with diamonds, de Beers prolonged the war. By months, or years, who knows? How many dead could be attributed to their greed. Fifty million dead in Europe in seven years. Diamonds played a large part. Diamonds and blood. Blood and diamonds. Did the British do anything with their backs against the wall? No, members of the London Diamond Exchange said there were plenty of diamonds. When Churchill and Roosevelt tried to intervene, they were told by Oppenheimer that industry had plenty of diamonds. The company has huge resources, enough to corrupt governments, agencies and officials in any country in the world.

The Rhodes scholarship, that is given to bright young students to study at Oxford, is supported by de Beers to influence the elite that sit on the boards of directors of large corporations, or have high positions in government.

I had a half Jewish grandmother, and my family disappeared into the camps. Since I had fought with the French and was a skilled machinist I avoided the camps, but I could not avoid seeing the boxes of industrial diamonds in the Krupp factory."

The little man finally fell silent, seemingly exhausted by his words and memories. They watched the cub playing in the leaves and attacking beetles. Lewis was thinking of his friends who had been killed by Nazi weapons. By his own hand Joseph had been forced to make the breech blocks of the deadly .88s of the German Panzers that terrorized the Allied infantry. Lewis had killed German soldiers, but he did not hate them. They were just doing their job, but he didn't lose all of his family like Joseph did.

Finally Lewis decided that it was time to come to the point.

"Joseph, why am I here and what do you want me to give to Marie?" Josephs head snapped back as if he was waking up from a nightmare.

"Marie cannot come to the Congo. The company knows that she has been collecting documents about the Nazi source of diamonds. She will have an 'accident,' and I cannot leave the country as they have stolen my passport, and will not issue me another." Lewis sighed.

"What good am I, Joseph? I was just a crazy man with a tiger, except that I was seen talking to you. Now I will be watched and will probably not be allowed out of the country." Joseph hung his head,

"I'm not a very good spy Lewis, but when we get back to the house, we will work out a plan."

As they were nearing the house Lewis stopped. He had never approached a house or building without reconnaissance in enemy territory, and this was enemy territory. Joseph fidgeted, wanting to hurry, and Lewis told him to hold the cub and be still. They had approached the house from the rear, and about five minutes later a light plume of smoke drifted around the corner from the veranda. Lewis moved to the other side of the house, and stepped to the side of the veranda. He found two men leaning against the wall near the door and smoking.

He motioned with the P-38 for them to move off the veranda and get on the ground, then called Joseph to come over. He asked Joseph if he knew them. Joseph shook his head no. He asked the white man who he was and what was he doing here, and when he did not reply, he shot him in the knee. When the black man turned to run, Lewis shot him in the head. He asked the writhing man the same questions again, and was answered in a torrent of French. The men were employees of the mining company. Joseph had been seen coming out of the concession and they were following him to see if he contacted anyone. The man asked for a doctor, and Lewis shot him. Joseph looked at the dead men and shrugged. He had seen executions before.

While Lewis fed the cub, Joseph went out to his small garden and dug up a steel box wrapped in oilskin. He told Lewis that it contained documents, a long letter to Marie, and a rough diamond the size of a small potato.

"It's from number 15. The company found 10 and I found 5. I reported the strike but not the diamond. I found part of it sticking out of the ground while I was eating my lunch. At first I couldn't believe anything that size could be a diamond. But it was."

They discussed the plan which was simple. Run. While Lewis stripped the bodies, and stuffed them under the house, Joseph packed. No memorabilia, he did not have any. Lewis packed his K Bar, spare ammo for the P-38, a bottle of goat's milk and a change of clothes. He had five spare eyes in his bag. He did not like kids lifting up his patch, and always kept an eye in. It also cooled women down looking into a gaping socket. He would scratch his glass eye on occasion just to watch people grit their teeth. He had fun with his handicap.

They waited until nightfall, and then walked to the train station. It was three hundred miles to the Capitol in Brazzaville, and since seventy percent of the population lived in the Capitol, or Point Norie, it would be possible for them to disappear until the bodies were found. Unfortunately Lewis received the same reception in Brazzaville as in Point Norie and he was mobbed by the crowd. Since Lewis stood out like a beacon in a population that was ninety-eight percent black, he told Joseph the plan would not work. Joseph, being a Belgian, having a skilled trade and the ability to speak French, could find work and blend in with the small white minority. Lewis would head for the hills and soldier it out, a trade he knew best.

Joseph was adamant that he would not leave his friend. Lewis finally told him if they stuck together they would both be killed and Marie would not get her box. Joseph reluctantly agreed. Lewis gave him the dead Frenchman's Beretta and half of Vinnie's money, and Joseph gave him the steel box. They silently shook hands. They had been together for only a short time, but in that time they had bonded like brothers.

Lewis changed his dollars for franks and bought a pack and some supplies in Brazzaville and started east into the vast interior of Africa. The Kongo were the largest ethnic group in the Congo, and spoke mostly Bantu. As he walked he started picking up the language from the children and the curious and friendly natives. White men rarely walked in Africa, but Lewis wanted to feel, smell and taste the continent that he had dreamed of seeing since he was a child. He was very happy and his only irritation was the occasional clank of the steel box. He had made the men of the 12th ROK regiment walk twenty-five miles a day with full packs and he marched with them. He couldn't do it on three rice balls a day, like the Inmun Gun, but they were fanatics.

THE EVIL EYE

22

As he walked further into the interior he started to see Pygmies, which were a small minority in the Congo. They were a jungle dwelling people, who had been ill treated by the invading Bantus. They had been considered sub-human, and were enslaved and sometimes eaten like animals.

Lewis encountered one of the little people in a small village where he stopped to buy some fruit. The pygmy was trading some honey for bread, and when he looked at the small pile of bread, he shook his head. Then the farmer removed two pieces from the small pile. Lewis had already paid the farmer for his bread, and quickly turned his back, reached in his pocket and switched eyes. He lifted the patch, turned back to the farmer and held up four fingers and pointed to the small pile. The shaking farmer put four pieces back on the pile. Lewis lowered the eye patch, and politely asked the farmer to sell him a bottle of goat's milk. The farmer returned with the milk and Lewis paid him twice the asking price. He thanked the now smiling farmer and walked back to the road, followed by the pygmy.

He twittered in a language that Lewis couldn't understand, and then asked in Bantu if he could see the eye. Reluctantly Lewis raised the patch, and the little man laughed, clapped his hands and disappeared into the bush. After an hour, Lewis stopped to feed the cub. He heard a slight sound and the same small man materialized out of the dense foliage. He asked in Bantu if they could see the eye, and his wife and children appeared as if by magic. Lewis complied, and they laughed and clapped. One small boy twittered something, probably a question, and Lewis twittered back in the same language. They looked at him in astonishment, and all started asking questions that Lewis couldn't answer. Finally he held up his hand with the thumb and index finger a quarter of an inch apart and said in Bantu, "A little." The father understood, and his little family smiled at Lewis and disappeared. Apparently some people were not intimidated by the "evil eye."

Pop wandered around Africa for two years or longer; he was always a bit vague about this period of his life. He was fluent in Bantu by then, but the land and language were changing. The cub was walking most of the time, but like most cats he lacked endurance, and Pop had to carry him the last few miles before they camped.

One day he came across a hunting camp, and the hunters seemed friendly and invited him to share their fire and spend the night. He was a light sleeper, and like his beloved tigers, he was instantly awake and alert when he heard a slight sound. The "friendly" hunters were creeping towards him. He lifted his patch, and the evil eye glowed red in the light of the dying campfire. The would-be assassins screamed and fled, dropping their machetes and leaving the rest of their gear behind. Pop said they probably still have stretch marks on their faces.

He noticed that the small groups of natives he encountered avoided him, and sometimes ran away. Only the old men would talk to him, and mostly in sign language. One very old man pointed to his patch. He raised it up and the old fellow nodded his head as if to say "Yup its true." They talked for over an hour, with gestures, shrugs, stick figures in the dirt and grimaces of pain. Finally the old man grabbed his own throat, staggered around, and fell to the ground.

Then Lewis understood. He was thought to be some kind of evil Shaman. A giant with an evil eye that could kill at a distance. Lewis reached in his pocket and gave the old man an extra green eye that he didn't use. The wizened face looked at the eye, and a yellow fingernail scratched the glass. He looked at the eye in his hand then looked at the evil eye. Then started shaking and turning blue. He was laughing so hard he couldn't breathe, and Lewis had to pound him on the back to get air into the old lungs.

Lewis consulted the map in his head and calculated that he was in the Central African Republic. The people still spoke Bantu or French, or some other dialect. He planned to push through CAR then swing through Nigeria to Niger.

There were a few big rivers to cross, like the Niger, but there ought to be some kind of ferry or boat. He marched through CAR like a Prussian Grenadier only stopping to buy food and sealed bottled water. The French had built good roads and he made it across the country in six weeks.

He swung northwest into Nigeria, and on the second day he stopped at a little stall on the side of the road where a little fat woman was frying some kind of vegetable with some kind of meat. She filled his plate, and asked where he got the lion cub. Lewis said it was a tiger cub and only ate cute little cooks. She giggled and they kidded around while he ate. A blind man passed the stall led by a small boy. Lewis had seen another blind man that day, so he asked the little cook about the blindness. She stopped smiling and told him that it was called "river blindness," as it was prevalent around large rivers. She also told him that the French said that it was caused by the bite of the black fly. Lewis gave her a very big tip. Good info is worth a good tip.

He turned around and headed back into CARs. Fear in combat is normal, panic is fatal. Fear of blindness is normal, but for Lewis it was fatal. He would never live blind, he would kill himself first.

He would avoid the water and the black fly, by going north to Chad, then swinging into the north end of Niger. He stopped in the town of Mao to have some new boots made and buy food and water. He also took a much needed bath, and washed his clothes.

They headed across Northern Niger heading to the Air

Mountains, a huge range in a sea of Sahel. To the North, part of the range was in the Sahara desert, and almost devoid of plant and animal life—and the black fly. He aimed for the Air Mountains but the compass in his head was faulty, and he got lost. He saw a group of cone shaped peaks in the distance and figured about forty miles. In the Sahara, distances can be deceiving, and the peaks were more than eighty miles away.

It was the young tiger that saved them. Lewis was on his last legs. The water was gone, no food left, and only his iron will kept him going. He was getting ready to start crawling, when the tiger trotted ahead and started digging. He looked into the tiny hole and saw a damp spot. He started enlarging the hole with his K Bar and soon they had a cupful of water. The tiger lapped it up and Pop got the second cup. The sun had dropped over the horizon by the time their thirst was quenched.

A prisoner of the Chinese had told him that if you had the will to survive you would and if you didn't you wouldn't. They had survived, but just barely. With the cat leading towards the peaks, and finding water every few miles, they neared their goal. The closer they came, the shallower the holes had to be dug for water, and the faster the pace. Large boulders surrounded the peaks, and the young tiger flattened to the ground. Pop froze; the cat had spotted something edible. The tiger crept closer and leaped behind a large boulder. Whatever it was, Pop skinned it out and they ate the meat, guts, broke the bones and sucked the marrow. Then rested in the shade of the peaks. The next day they walked towards the base of the peaks, and rounding a large boulder they almost ran over a young woman. And she was white.

Lewis was absolutely stunned speechless. The woman was young, blond, beautiful, and buck naked. She screamed and ran like a deer to a camp that looked to Lewis like a pile of tin. When other nude white men and women emerged from the camp he knew he was hallucinating. In retrospect he couldn't blame the woman from running. A huge, ugly one eyed man with a patch, tangled hair and a beard garnished with bits of blood and skin would scare the wits out of a plaster saint. He sat down and looked at the ground with his head in his hands. Ten minutes later he looked up and they were still there watching him. He relaxed. However improbable they were real.

In a few minutes an older man, about fifty, walked up and asked him in French who he was and how he'd gotten here. Lewis replied that he was Sergeant Major Lewis Sergeant of the United States army, and that he had walked here. The man obviously did not believe the "walked" part. Lewis asked a question of his own. "Why are all of you." he paused, and the man smiled and said,

"Naked? Because we have no clothes, they all rotted away." Then he asked Lewis why he carried a gun. Lewis lied and told him it was army regulations, then added, "I'm sorry to have frightened the young woman."

"Sharia" the man interjected. "Walk with me to out home."

When they arrived, the leader, Jacques introduced Lewis to the other seventeen members of the group. When he got to Sharia, there were two of them. Identical twins, and until one of them spoke not even their mother could tell them apart. Lewis immediately forgot their names; he always remembered them as the "Gold Dust Twins."

THE GOLD DUST TWINS / 1957-1990

23

They were shy at first, with Lewis having clothes and them being nude. Then, in typical French fashion, they all started talking at once. Jacques raised his hand. "One at a time please," then asked the first question. "Did France go to war?" Puzzled, Lewis asked him which war was he talking about, and was astonished when Jacques said,

"With the Germans." Lewis counted back in his head and calculated that this group had been here since 1937 or '38.

He told them about the World War II from the French viewpoint. The war had started with the invasion of Poland, the defeat of France, and the British, the victorious march through Paris led by General de Gaulle, and the final defeat of Germany. One of the twins asked about the fashions in Paris, and another about the town of Rimes. Lewis had been in the hospital in Rimes, and when the man asked about advances in medical procedures, Lewis knew he was a doctor.

When the questions petered out, the little group was silent, digesting the events that had happened in the world in the last twenty years. Lewis asked Jacques if anyone had a razor or a scissors so he could shave and cut his hair. The mother of the twins volunteered. Her name was Darnell, a tall graceful woman with black hair and sad grey eyes. With the twins watching to see what kind of face would emerge from the wilderness, she expertly cut his hair and shaved his beard.

When she finished, he asked her what kind of tip she wanted. She smiled and replied that a black evening dress and shoes with four inch heels would do. Darnell was in her mid forties but looked ten years younger. She was not beautiful like her daughters, but had a striking face and athletic body.

That evening they had a surprisingly good meal of chicken, potatoes and some type of greens. Lewis gave half his plate to the hungry tiger before he killed something or someone. That morning the tiger had gone out to hunt and returned without success. The cat was almost two years old and much thinner from their trek across the desert. He was creeping up on a chicken, and Lewis was ready to stop him, when Jacques said,

"Let him go, we can't catch the thing anyway." The wary rooster paused to peck at a bug and was dead in an instant. The tiger trotted behind a boulder to eat his kill. Jacques and everyone else, who had seen the action, were impressed. That night he went on the prowl, and when he returned the next day he lay down beside Lewis and threw up a large hairball. Lewis called him hairball the rest of his life.

Lewis asked Jacques if he could explore around the camp or home as the people called it. Jacques said he would go with him. Lewis did not trust the cat around the chickens and took him with them. They walked to a huge fissure in the rock, and Lewis saw the remains of what looked like an old Junker tri-motor and realized why the camp was built out of tin. The sides and wings had been removed to build the camp. Jacques saw the flash of understanding on his face as they walked to the shade of a huge boulder and sat down. Jacques said that they had been there so long that they had almost forgotten how it came to be;

"We had been sent by our church to aid a town in Niger that had been infected by Typhus. The plane was packed with twenty missionaries and with crates of chickens, three pigs, medical supplies, some food and three boxes of goods that our mission in the town had requested. We fueled the plane in Brazzaville and headed to the Air Mountains. When we got to the mountains, the pilot said we were on the wrong side, so we turned west and were caught in a sandstorm. When we climbed out of the storm, we couldn't see anything. We were running low on fuel, so the pilot dropped the plane near the ground to see where we were. We had braced ourselves for a rough landing, and when we saw the boulders on the ground it was too late

143

to pull up. We bounced off this boulder and crashed into the fissure."

Jacques sighed and shook his head.

"Lord what a mess, chickens squawking, pigs squealing and blood and feathers all over. The pilot was killed and the co-pilot was barely alive and died two days later. Five of us were unhurt and pulled the rest out of the plane. Doctor Pare' was not hurt except for a gash in his head, and with Darnell's help he patched up the survivors. Darnell's husband was out cold and woke up with a concussion and a headache."

Lewis asked how they had managed to stay alive in this … he almost said god-forsaken, but changed it to desolate place. Jacques said that they were missionaries, and did not come only to treat Typhus.

"We have men and women with different skills, and we bought pigs and chickens to upgrade the local stock, and drought resistant seeds to make life better for the people. On the other side of this peak, there is a wadi, and we found a pool of water. The old man, Thomas, is a genius an inventor and can fix anything, except a radio," he added ruefully.

"We had plenty of sand and mixed up with chicken manure, night soil, and pig blood, we made a garden, and watered it with tin cans until Thomas made a windmill from the wreckage, and a hose from a fuel line. It took time and we had to kill the pigs and most of the chickens, except for one very fertile rooster and three hens. There were tools in the plane, and when we opened the boxes for the mission we found more tools, a box of yarn, and a box of canned tuna. It was a very close thing. Until the chicks grew up and the garden started producing we almost starved."

Lewis wanted to look at the wreck and Jacques went with him. They heard a banging sound and a curse and Thomas emerged from the wreckage sucking his bruised thumb. His hair was snow white from his pubis to the top of his head.

"Thomas you used the Lords name in vain again, and I will not tolerate blasphemy in our community." Thomas hung his head in shame, but turned and gave Lewis a sly wink.

"I was trying to get a pipe out but the spanner slipped." Lewis crawled into the plane and hit the big bolt with a hammer, and removed the nut with the wrench.

"What are you making now?"

"Two shovels for those darn kids. Making the pond bigger will take some of the p— ah … vinegar out of them."

After dinner, it was story time and, since they had heard each others stories a thousand times they all focused on Lewis. Lewis tried to keep out the gory parts of what he had seen and done and told them about the fashions. The Paris women and their four-inch spiked heels, hairstyles, but leaving out the parts about the low cleavages and prostitution.

"What are spiked heels?" Asked one of the twins. Lewis looked at Darnell, and she told them that they were shoes that made women taller and their calves look fuller. Jacques asked about Germany.

"We bombed Berlin to rubble," he said with relish.

"But what about innocent civilians, they didn't kill anyone."

"They killed fifty million people," Lewis said harshly, and then told them about the death camps at Dachau and Auschwitz.

"Almost everyone knew what was happening," he said bitterly, "and only a few tried to stop the slaughter. They killed my friends and worked thousands of Russians to death in their factories. You people are missionaries, remember what Amald Amharic said when asked by his Generals as what to do about the mix of Catholics and Cathars in the City of Beziers? 'Kill them all. God will know his own', and that applied to the Berliners." Lewis looked and saw the shocked look in the faces of those gentle people.

"I'm sorry I just got carried away, but there are evil people in this world, and you should know the truth." Finally, Thomas broke the silence.

"Thank you Lewis, it's hard to relive the past, and I, for one, appreciate your honesty"

The weeks passed peacefully for Lewis. He helped the twins enlarge the pond by building a dam with rocks. The were young, graceful and very strong. They were also very inquisitive.

"Lewis, why do you bathe at night, and never take off your clothes?" Lewis had been waiting for that one.

"I have a very sensitive skin and sunlight gives me a bad rash." The younger twin, by a few seconds, looked at him doubtfully,

"Then why are your hands and face brown?" Lewis thought for a minute. *I don't want to lie to these kids. They are too damned smart, too innocent and trusting, besides I really like them.*

"The skin is the largest organ of the human body and subject to several ailments such as rashes and genetic conditions. Piebald Spotting, is genetic whereas rashes like mine is a Contact Dermatitis, and the cause is sunlight." He laughed,

"Maybe I have a 'Farmer Tan.'"

"What's a farmer tan?"

"Anyone that works all day in the hot sun with a long shirt on gets a brown face, and when he takes off his shirt he has a brown V on his neck to match his face. He usually has a snow white body. The twins seemed satisfied with that evasion, and they finished enlarging the pond.

Lewis also helped Thomas strip parts from the plane, attended church meetings on Sunday, taking comfort in the testaments of the people. Nevertheless, he felt that he should be doing more to earn his keep. One day he decided to scale the peak and have a look around. When he reached the top, he sat on a rock and looked west. In the far distance, he saw what looked like a small mound. As the sun rose higher, he could see that it was definitely a mound with what looked like bushes or trees on top. He marked the spot from where the sun set and climbed down from the peak. The mound was not visible from ground level but

147

he knew where it was.

THE LONG WAY HOME

24

The next day he filled every bottle in camp with water and filled his pack. He left the steel box with Darnell. When she asked where he was going, he said just for a look around. He saw a tear in her eye.

"That's what my husband said and he never came back." When the sun set Lewis marked the spot and he and the tiger headed for the mound. It had looked like forty or fifty miles but he had been fooled before. They walked at a fast pace and when the sun rose, he saw that the mound was closer than he thought. He saw what appeared to be a small tree a mile away. When they got there, they rested in its meager shade.

As the sun was setting, he heard a small snort from the tiger. He did not move and slowly opened his eye, and saw a large male Gazelle followed by three females and a calf. They were four hundred yards away, and moving towards the tree. The tiger was crouching, and ready to give chase, but Lewis hissed at him and he flattened down. There were no predators in this desolate part of Niger and the animals were curious. At three hundred yards, Lewis slowly drew the P-38 and at a hundred yards, he shot the male in the chest. He gutted the animal and gave the liver and heart to the tiger. He skinned it, while the tiger lapped up the blood from the cavity.

Lewis had calculated four bottles out and five back if they were unsuccessful. Therefore, they drank most of the water and started back to camp. The carcass weighed over two hundred pounds and they had to slow down the pace. One of the twins saw a figure in the distance, and as he got closer, she saw that it was Lewis, carrying a carcass. She ran back to camp screaming "meat, meat." Back in camp, Lewis washed his bloody shirt and watched the people cutting up the carcass. They had not seen that much red meat since they killed the last pig over twenty years ago.

Thomas was slicing small thin strips for drying and bigger chunks for baking in the solar oven he had built. He looked at Lewis and said,

"Lord thank you for this bounty." Then he added under his breath, "Because I'm farting feathers from a diet of chicken."

That evening Jacques took Lewis aside. He had a gleam in his eye, and asked if this may be a way out. Lewis gave him a thoughtful look, and said,

"It would be easy to get to the mound, but after that I don't know. I would need two or three strong men to help carry water and food, but I'm willing to try"

Jacques called the people together and told them the plan. When he came to the part about needing three strong men the twins threw a "rigging fit" in logging parlance, or a conniption in English.

"We're stronger than you old farts," one said, and the other chipped in with

"And a heck of a lot tougher too." Jacques looked around for support, and finding none, he weakly said that it was up to their mother. Darnell told him that she was going with them.

They started out the next evening loaded down with food and water. Lewis carried his pistol and K-Bar, a load of water, and set a fast pace. It was sunup when they reached the small tree and the drying hide underneath. They rested under a sun that blazed like the fires of hell. The next night they had walked five or six miles, when the tiger gave a small snort and loped ahead disappearing into the darkness. They pressed ahead following the tiger. As the sun slowly rose, they saw the cat crouched at the edge of a wadi.

Lewis motioned for the women to stop and he walked silently to where the tiger was crouched. When he looked into the wadi, he saw the same small herd of gazelle grazing on a patch of grass near a small pool of water. The cat softly crept down the slope, freezing when one of the gazelles lifted its head. When it dropped its head to graze, the cat rushed and sprang, killing the animal without a sound.

The mound was only a few hundred yards from the wadi

and Lewis walked up to have a look around. The base of the hill was covered with dry branches and when he got closer, he found a small seam of coal. Using his K-Bar, he pried chunks of coal from the seam and stuffed his pack full. Carrying an armload of branches, he returned to the sleeping women. He ground the dry leaves into powder and cut slivers from the branches. Pulling the slug from the casing of a bullet, he carefully poured the powder on the crushed leaves. Then with the back of his knife, he struck sparks from a rock. After several tries, a spark hit the gunpowder and ignited the leaves and slivers. He added pieces of wood and small chunks of coal as the fire grew, and the hotter it got, the larger the chunks. Despite the noise he made banging on the rock, the sleeping women did not wake up until they smelled roasting meat.

"My God, Lewis where is the salad," Darnell said. The spit was full of roasted meat, and when they'd eaten their fill, they roasted the rest for the days of hunger ahead. The tiger seemed pleased with himself, and lay down and slept. Lewis climbed back to the seam and brought back more coal, then went to bed behind two rocks that had retained the day's heat.

Using his pack for a pillow, he was almost asleep when Darnell lay beside him and put her head on his chest. She looked at him and whispered,

"I haven't had a man in seventeen years."

"Its probably grown shut by now," Lewis quipped, and got a sharp poke in the ribs as a reply.

"Maybe you can crack it open for me," she said, unbuttoning his shirt, while he began to stroke her breasts. She removed his boots, and slid off his pants. When she saw his body, she gasped.

"My God Lewis did you get run over by a train?"

"Just a few Chinese, come on over here and lets fool around a bit. She climbed on, and they fooled around until Darnell's heavy breathing indicated that she was through fooling around.

Darnell was a noisy lover, although she tried to keep quiet for fear of waking the twins. They made love most of the night, and finally Darnell lay on his chest, the sweat cooling on her back.

"I hope those brats haven't been watching," she said. *God forbid* Lewis thought.

"You have a beautiful body, and a healthy set of lungs. They should be hanging down to your navel with those two kids sucking on them."

"I nursed them for two years, the poor little things were always hungry," she mused. "Jacques always found an extra can of tuna for me and I fed them bits of tuna and chewed up chicken like baby birds." They heard the twins moving around, and Darnell moved to the fire and chewed on a chunk of meat. The twins looked at their mother and asked sarcastically if she had slept well.

The twins had been watching their mother writhe on the organ that had deeply penetrated her body. "How can she take that thing," the youngest asked her sister. Her twin

153

was rocking herself with the movements of her mother, and answered with a groan. They had been masturbating since puberty, but technically they were still virgins, although reluctant ones and their silky bottoms were keeping metronomic time with their mothers.

Darnell knew that her girls were watching and what they were doing, and smiled to herself. *They had to learn some time* she thought as a wave of passion surged over her and she collapsed on the body of her lover. Her husband had been a gentle lover and she had orgasms before, but not the explosive kind that seemed to rock her body forever.

They climbed the small hill and found an outcrop where they had a clear view of the trail ahead. There was a line of hills at least a hundred miles ahead and nothing in between but rock and sand.

"We had better rest tonight and leave tomorrow night. It's about a four night march, and not much shade, so drink lots of water before we go"

Just before they reached the bottom of the hill one of the twins let out a squawk. She sat on a rock and examined a large scratch above her blond pubic hair. She looked at Lewis innocently and said,

"Kiss it daddy and make it all well."

Lewis turned beet red, and the women laughed until their sides hurt.

Lewis had made a rough pack out of the hide, and carried the meat and a haunch for the cat. They walked all night, and tried to rest while the sun beat down on them like a hammer. The next two days were the same, and by the fourth day they were still several miles from the hills. Lewis marveled at the stamina of the women, who trudged on without complaint. The fifth night they reached the hills and collapsed completely exhausted.

Lewis got up, and taking the tiger with him, he went looking for water. He found a trickle coming from a small spring and filled their bottles. They drank their fill and returned to the women, who immediately drank three full bottles. Lewis was sleeping, but woke up when he heard a strange sound. He looked up and saw the tiger dragging a goat.

Well he thought *this is good news and bad news. The good news is that a goat means that there are people around; ergo some sort of town or village is near. The bad news is that this is Muslim country, and the men want their women covered from head to foot and veiled, not naked with their tits flopping around. In addition, the owner of the goat will want payment.*

He told the women to hide and stay quiet. Then he and the tiger went looking for the owner of the goat. Down a track, he saw a small boy tending a band of goats followed by an old man and two women. He walked up to the man and made the universal sign of peace. He asked the man in Bantu if he spoke the language. By the puzzled look on his face, he did not. Hopefully he asked the man if he spoke French. The man's face brightened and he said, "Just a little." With a little pointing, and some French, Lewis told them that his tiger killed one of their goats. The grandson

155

understood first and told the old man the story in Hausa. The man laughed, and said in broken French,

"Goat is pig eat woman cloths." Lewis offered to pay for the goat and pulled a bill from his watch pocket. The man looked at the bill then looked sharply at Lewis.

"You no French," he said. "French no pay nothing,"

"American," Lewis said, and the old man replied,

"Go with Allah, American," and walked away.

Lewis asked the boy if there was a village nearby. The boy made an arc over his head and pointed down the path. Lewis thanked him and walked back to the women. He sat down looking dejected, then looked up at their worried faces.

"We made it," he said with a huge grin. They had gambled with their lives and won.

Lewis and Hairball walked to the village leaving the women hidden out of sight. In two hours, they reached a small village near an oasis. The American and the tiger attracted a crowd immediately. One small boy asked what kind of animal it was, and Lewis said it was a Bengal Tiger. The boy asked what it ate.

"Just little boys." The kid laughed and asked to pet him. Lewis nodded and the boy started stroking his fur. A young man asked him in perfect French, if he was lost.

"No" Lewis said, "but I need to buy some clothing for my wife and daughters. A goat ate all their clothes." Some people laughed at that.

"Probably Djibo's goat, he eats everything," someone said.

The young man led Lewis to a small store, and he picked out three black dresses for his 'family' and held out a frank note for payment. The man shook his head; he did not have enough change. Lewis told him he would return with his family, as they needed some supplies.

The twins were excited with their new clothing. Darnell looked sad as she watched her children prance around in those cheap dresses. They had been naked since birth, and these black rags were their first dresses. Lewis saw the sadness and quietly told her that it was the best he could do.

"You're a good man Lewis," and kissed him on the cheek.

Lewis told the women that they must always walk behind him, carry everything and not speak to any man; eye contact is okay but not to overdo it. Darnell ask why a man needed his hands free.

"It's a holdover from the days when men had a sword in one hand and a shield in the other," Lewis replied. "The men walked in front to protect the women."

They entered the small store, and the twins acted as if it was Macy's. They looked at the cheap rings and trinkets as if they were diamonds and rubies, and in their innocent eyes, they were. Darnell looked at Lewis and he nodded, so she told the girls they could each have one. This took about an hour, and as they were leaving the young French speaker walked in. The innocent look vanished from the twin's eyes, as they looked him over. Lewis introduced his family, and Darnell thanked him for his help. Lewis asked him where the nearest town was with an airport.

"That would be Chufa, its twenty-five miles from here and you would pass through the abandoned town of Djado, but you can get water there."

FOUR BAGS OF GOLD

25

They walked towards the town of Djado and by sundown, they had reached the crumbling walls of the ancient city. The city had a small population, mostly transients, and Lewis told them not to wander off, as they might be kidnaped. A tall thin Arab trader asked Lewis if he would sell one of the twins and offered him a small bag of gold.

"One is worth more than that, at least two bags," Lewis countered. The twins were getting interested in the transaction.

"And a blond virgin would be worth four bags, he added."

"I'll get the gold and bring it to you tonight," the Arab said as he walked away.

"I'm worth at least five bags since I'm the youngest," said one twin,

"But I'm more beautiful." said her identical sister.

"Cut out the crap," Lewis said. "Darnell, take the kids over to that patch of bushes, hide and don't make a sound.

That guy is going to try to kidnap the girls and he won't be alone. Take Hairball with you and don't be surprised if he disappears."

Lewis sat in the shadow of the wall and waited for the Arab to make his move.

At midnight, Lewis heard a faint scraping sound, and stepped around the corner of the wall, fired three quick shots and stepped back facing the other direction. The Arab was raising a rifle, and Lewis shot him in the head. *That's four,* he thought, and a horrible scream made five. He ran over to a man that had been gutted, and lay writhing on the ground. He snarled something to the cat, who was sniffing at the blood, and shot the man in the head. They walked over to the shocked women, and Lewis said "Pack up, we're going." He put a full clip in his Walther, put on the pack and started towards Chiffa. The women were almost running. Lewis told them to slow down and follow the tiger, and he fell back a hundred yards to cover the rear.

After ten miles, Lewis called a halt, and moved the women several yards off the track and behind a clump of brush. One of the twins was crying and Darnell was trying to comfort her. Darnell looked at him and asked,

"How did you know that man would try to kidnap the girls?"

"That scum wouldn't pay four bags of gold to save his mother, he's a slave trader and would have sold the girls to the highest bidder." The twin that had been crying said,

"Why did Hairball rip that man to shreds, and why did

you shoot him?"

"He probably had his arm covering his throat, so he just gutted him instead.

I shot the man to put him out of his misery, he wouldn't have lived anyway."

Lewis squatted beside the young girl.

"Honey, I told you once that there is evil in this world, and it is my job to protect my friends, my family and the people I love from that evil. Now get some rest. We're leaving in the morning."

Jean Moulin was an old Africa hand, and thought he had seen everything, until a one eyed man, three women and a tiger walked into his office. Darnell and the girls had bought new French clothes in Chirfa, and Darnell had won the argument over the cleavage factor. The new shoes hurt their feet as they had been barefoot most of their lives.

"Darnell, why don't you tell Mister Moulin why we are here, and if you do not mind, sir, I would like to look at your J-58."

The Junker and the Goony Bird, Lewis thought, *the workhorses of the world.* The plane looked well tended. The Junker could land and take off on short airstrips and carry a heavy load. The three engines gave it the power to lift and a good pilot could glide for miles on those wide wings if he knew his thermalis.

When he got back, he saw that Darnell was not making much headway with Jean, who was shaking his head. Darnell was losing her calm demeanor, and the twins were no help, just having fun egging their mother on. Jean knew the terrain and did not believe that three women could survive the trip, and he absolutely did not believe that seventeen people could survive twenty years in that God forsaken part of the Sahara.

Lewis asked him how much it would cost to fly him over to the camp, and if he could find a place to land, he would pay him double. The price was more than Lewis had, and he was a hundred franks short. He pulled out the Walther and handed it to Jean along with all the franks. Jean shook his head.

"Keep the gun; I'd only shoot myself in the foot."

When they reached cruising altitude, Jean switched on the radio. He called the military base at Agadez, and asked them if they had any information on a missing Junker with twenty missionaries in about 1937 or '38. Lewis smiled, *can't blame him for checking, I sure would.*

The voice said he would call back in twenty minutes. Thirty minutes later the voice came back, but was too garbled to understand. In another hour, Lewis spotted the small peak, and the Jean turned the plane slightly. When they buzzed the camp, people waved and cheered at them.

"Jesus, Mary and all the Saints, I guess I owe you an apology." Jean said, and Lewis grinned at him.

"I'll owe you several hundred more franks if you can find a place to land." Jean dropped the Junker in a clear spot so gently that Lewis could hardly tell they were on the ground. Lewis jogged to the camp where he was hugged and kissed by people who were delirious with joy. He was asked dozens of questions about the women, the journey and how they managed to survive. Jacques said with tears in his eyes.

"We thought you were dead, and we mourned and prayed for you for weeks."

Finally, Lewis told them to pack their things and get moving as they were burning daylight. The little group was silent. Thomas spoke up.

"Lewis, some of us aren't going. This is our home and most of our families in France are gone; this is our family now." Three of the men who might have grandchildren turned and went to collect their meager possessions.

"What about you Jacques", Lewis said. "You're a missionary without a mission, and a deacon without a church." Jacques closed his eyes in pain. He had been thinking the same thing that Lewis had put into words.

"I'm sorry Lewis, but I cannot leave my people." Lewis turned and started walking toward the plane.

"I'll be back with some supplies; if anyone else wants to leave they can be on the next flight."

When they were nearing Chirfa a voice came over the radio loud and clear.

"A plane did disappear in 1937 and the people were presumed dead."

"Well they're not dead, and I have three of them in my plane."

"That is not possible; no one could live in that place for twenty years."

163

"Well they did," Jean said, "over and out." "Damned bureaucrats," he muttered When they landed the men refused to leave the plane naked, and Jean brought them some old coveralls. There was a joyous reunion with the women that turned to sadness when they learned that the others were staying. Jean and Lewis left the office to give them some privacy. Lewis pulled out a wad of franks from his carryall and paid Jean.

"I'd like to hire you for a week or two, if you have the time." Jean agreed and Lewis paid him in advance.

"You're sure aren't a Frenchman," Jean said.

The following days were hectic for Lewis and if it had not been for Jean and Darnell, he would have been overwhelmed. Darnell picked out clothes for the people staying behind, and Jean bought food, books and other supplies that were on Darnels's list. Lewis was busy fielding calls from Niamey, Agadez and Paris. Trouble came by plane in the form of a tall lanky Frenchman, complete with pith helmet and swagger stick. He had a stack of forms and wanted to see the firearm permit, his passport, how he got to Niger, the importation of a dangerous animal, and so on.

In desperation, Lewis went to the office and called Marie. He told her his troubles, and Marie asked to speak to the official. In thirty seconds, the man's face went white, and he scurried out of the office leaving a trail of forms. Marie told Lewis that Joseph was dead, and choked up. When she could finally speak she said, "And I thought you were, too." Then she said briskly. "'I'll see you in Niamey."

and hung up.

Whatever she had said to the official worked and the calls ceased, except one from the French Embassy asking for his itinerary. Jean flew the supplies to the camp, and the only passenger that returned was Jacques. He kissed the women and handed Lewis a note from Thomas. *'Thank you my friend, and give the money to the girls.'*

He asked Jacques, "What money?"

"Didn't you know? Thomas won the Nobel Prize for Chemistry, and never bothered to collect the prize money."

When they arrived in Niamey, the gendarmes tried to keep the mob meeting them from the spinning props. Reporters, dignitaries, the mayor and the French minister of Colonial Affairs crowded around the door. The twins and the tiger stuck their heads out and the flashbulbs lit up the sky. The photo of the beautiful, wide-eyed twins and the fierce looking tiger was flashed around the world, and published on the covers of Life, Time and the National Geographic. The story had everything: survival and a dangerous journey across the hostile Sahara, naked women, a war hero, a Nobel Prize winner, a huge tiger and maybe a little sex to top it off. The reporters were salivating for the details. The minister led the survivors to the embassy, and the crowd finally dispersed.

Lewis had stayed in the plane, talking with Jean when the long arm of the CIA appeared in the form of a well dressed man. He politely asked Lewis if he would accompany him to a quiet hotel far away from the embassy. He added, when he saw the stubborn look on Lewis's face, that Marie would like to see him. Lewis gave Jean the rest of the franks, shook hands and he and the cat followed the agent to the hotel.

Marie met him at the door, hugged him, and kissed him on the cheek.

"That agent who just left is one of three that are here to watch our backs," she said. "de Beers knows you are alive and have Joseph's deposition and records of the sale of diamonds to the Nazis." Lewis pulled the steel box out of his carryall, gave it to Marie, and was not surprised when she produced a key. She opened the box and picked up a large object wrapped in cloth. Unwrapping it, she held up a large rough diamond, and read the deposition attached.

"Lewis, Joseph gave this rock to you. What do you want to do with it?"

"Cut a large, sharp diamond out of it so it will really hurt when I shove it up Oppenheimer's ass." Lewis snarled, still grieving over his friends death. Marie nodded and started to read the documents and Lewis and the tiger went into the spare bedroom. Lewis awoke feeling well rested, not knowing that it was going to be his last rest for quite some time,

Lewis did not recognize it yet but he was a very small fish in a very large pond. The president of the United States and the president of France were having a tiff. de Gaulle wanted his own nuclear deterrent, and the United States wanted France to join NATO. It was felt that Sergeant

Lewis Sergeant, who had been promised the Legion of Honor from de Gaulle's own hand, could improve the relationship between the two countries. De Gaulle had honestly forgotten about it and agreed to carry out his earlier promise. For Lewis, the thought of another medal ceremony was linked to the painful memory of Dominique who lay in an unmarked grave in France. Marie deserved the honor, Lewis didn't want it.

He had hitched a ride with Jean to Point Norie, and picked up a French newspaper with the headline, "Sex and Murder in Niger." Darnels' noisy passion had awakened the twins and they had indeed sneaked up to watch. Their vivid description of the tiger ripping the guts out of one of the killers, and Lewis finishing him off with a shot to the head, made Lewis livid. On the long voyage from Point Norie to Marseille he started to worry about the French Police.

He needn't have worried as the French *Suerte'* knew that the Arab was kidnapping young girls and selling them to wealthy Sultans as sex slaves. They had no proof, and Lewis had done them a favor. His urge to strangle the twins waned and he started to laugh about the two young blabbermouths. He also wanted to see Darnell again.

The first shot across his bow was a missive from the U.S. Secretary of State asking him to be in Paris for the medal ceremony. Lewis threw it away. The second telegraph was from the vice president telling him to be in Paris. Lewis thought the VP was a political hack and threw that one away too. The third and final message came from a four-star general telling him to haul ass to Paris or he would get his balls cut off. Lewis understood that one and hauled ass to Paris.

Pop always detested the hero business. The really brave were usually killed, and without several witnesses or an officer, they were put in the ground and forgotten

My father had gotten Darnell pregnant, and wanted to get married, but she turned him down. She did not want to leave France and he was in a high risk profession, and she did not want to lose another husband. Jacques wanted to marry her, pregnant or not, and she accepted him.

Lewis had one more duty to perform in Paris before he left France, and he was not looking forward to it. He was told by the army to wear his dress uniform, all his decorations and not to embarrass the army. He was big, scarred, ugly, and wore the evil eye under his patch. He was covered with decorations, with the screaming eagle patch on one shoulder and his sergeant majors rank on the other. The *Palais de l' Elysees* was jammed with ambassadors, ministers and other high officials, with a sprinkling of men in uniform. Two French paratroopers saw the screaming eagle patch and walked over to chat. They all agreed that the air attack at Normandy was a royal fuckup.

Darnell and the twins saw him through the crowd and ran over for kisses and hugs. While the twins were hugging him, one of them looked up, and when Lewis turned his head, a flashbulb went off in his face. (The photo made the front page under the caption "Beauty and the Beast.".

When de Gaulle saw the photo he was furious. He called the editor and chewed him to ribbons. The next day the paper printed a long apology).

De Gaulle and his minions arrived and the ceremony began. De Gaulle's 'minions' were not the usual dignitaries that surround a head-of-state. As a consequence of several attempts on his life, the men were heavily armed ex- paratroops. The four recipients lined up and the French president went down the line, bussing the man on the cheeks and chatting with each, before he pinned on the award. Lewis had removed the patch, and the evil red eye shown in all its glory. De Gaulle looked Lewis in the eye and smiled.

"You probably scared the hell out of a lot of recruits with that one." He pinned on the medal, and said, "Thank you for the service to our country, Sergeant Major." Lewis replied,

"It was an honor to fight with so many brave men and women" They saluted, and de Gaulle turned and walked away.

He ducked out the back door and went to the best hotel on the *Rue du Faibourg* where each one of the famous survivors and Lewis had been given magnificent suites. Lewis had even been allowed to keep his furry pet with him. Darnell answered the door in her nightgown. She had taken off her dress and had been brushing her hair. Lewis bent down and kissed her ear, and fondled her breasts. She aroused faster than any woman he had ever known.

In thirty seconds they were on the bed, one minute to re-move their clothes, ten seconds of foreplay and he was in.

She yelled, screamed and drummed her heels on his back. She had always tried to hold back with the twins around, but this time she let it all out. After two hours of violent sex they were exhausted, and Lewis figured that he would be pissing blood for a week.

"I'm going to miss you Lewis, and I will always love you," she said, "So please go so I can have a good cry."

The girls had listened to their mother's passionate screaming from their suit and felt frustrated. They snuck into Lewis's room and hid in the closet. The Bengal watched them enter and ignored them. Lewis came in slightly drunk and depressed at being rejected by Darnel and flopped down and went to sleep. He always slept in boxer shorts, and had fallen into a deep sleep after the ex-hausting session with Darnell. The twins silently slipped into the bed and and were gently trying to unbutton his shorts when Lewis reared up, pistol in hand to see the two frightened girls. His initial reaction was rage, and the look in his eye quenched their lust instantly. Lewis deeply loved the golden haired twins, the daughters of his lover, and he considered them family. The twins thought of him as a lover, not as a father, a mistake that he would quickly rec-tify. He picked them up and draped them over the end of the bed, with their golden rears face up, and proceeded to turn the gold into bright red until his hand was sore. The tears were streaming down their faces, but except for a few grunts, the twins were silent. Lewis picked them up, got into bed, and tucked the girls in on each side.

"I love you both more than life itself, including your mother," he said. "And I will always be there to love and protect you. When you get married I will give you away, and your children will be my grandchildren." He kissed the tears from their eyes, and they snuggled up to him and slept.

The next morning, Lewis called Marie before the twins were awake. He asked her if she would keep an eye on the girls when he was away. She told him to bring them over for a get-to know-you session. On the drive over Lewis told the girls all about his best friend. The girls were fascinated by her life history and were wide-eyed about Marie's male equipment. They had met Marie once, and had been awed by the woman's grace and beauty, and found it hard to believe, even from Lewis, that she was a sexual male. When they arrived at Maries, she told Lewis to go do something for the army, because she and the twins were going shopping.

If the war had not interfered, Marie would have been one of the top fashion designers of women's clothing in Paris. She enjoyed dressing the girls, and was impressed by their beauty and acuity. The twins had received an excellent education from Thomas and the other missionaries, and under Marie's guidance they learned when to curb their normal boisterous behavior and act like sophisticated Parisian women.

Darnel welcomed Maries help, as she was going through a long bout of morning sickness, and the twins were a handful even when she wasn't sick. Like most women, Darnel needed a woman confidant, and Maire was a good listener. Darnel told her of her daughter's quest to lose their virginity, and she was worried that they would give it up to some French swordsman with a good line of bullshit.

Lewis had told Marie of the girls attempt to use him as their instrument of de-flowerment, so she told Darnel. Darnel laughed so hard that she got sick and had to go vomit.

"Now that they have stopped fixating on Lewis," Darnel said when she returned white-faced, "I'd better get them fitted for diaphragms".

"Those things won't protect them from VD." Marie said. "You've been isolated too long. There are a lot of bad bugs being passed around in the sex department." They agreed to get together and work out a plan.

While Marie and Darnel were working out a plan for the girls, the twins were working out a plan for Marie, and the next day they cornered her when she got home from work. They had prepared a light supper for her and heavy on the wine. Marie knew they were up to something and waited for the plot to unfold. The oldest fired the first salvo with flattery.

"Marie, you are the only one that treats as adults instead of children. Mother and pappa still treat us like teenagers and pappa even spanked us." she concluded indignantly.

"But Marie," said her sister, "we are women and we need to feel what it is like to have a man inside of us, instead of playing with ourselves like children."

Marie saw where the conversation was heading, and remembering Jeanette, she closed her eyes and shuddered. The twins, seeing that something they had said caused her pain, cuddled her with kisses and soft words of endearment. Their obvious concern for her suffering drew out the story of Marie's relationship with Jeanette and the pain and guilt that still remained.

"I'm afraid I can't help you young women lose your virginity." Marie said, "I used one young woman and I will never use another." The youngest gave her an age-old smile and kissed her softly on the lips.

"You won't be using us," she said, "We'll be using you."

With an almost clinical detachment, Marie watched the seduction of her body. The oldest removed Mares dress and underclothes, while the youngest removed her own clothing slowly and seductively for Marie's enjoyment When the younger twin effortlessly swallowed Mares tumescent organ, Marie wondered how long she had been practicing. They worked like a well oiled team of football players heading for the goal line, and Marie finally got off the bench and joined the team.

The next morning, while the sated twins slept, Marie woke up and staggered to the kitchen and made herself a cup of coffee. After the second cup, she braced herself and called Darnel.

"You'll probably hate me for this," she said. "But it wasn't my idea." Darnel broke in.

"The little shits seduced you, didn't they?"

The army brass was pleased by Lewis's behavior at the ceremony in Paris. Their highly decorated sergeant was sometimes considered a loose cannon, and they let out a collective sigh of relief when the presentation ceremony went smoothly.

Lewis went back to his family in Oregon for a long visit. His parents were in their seventies and both his brothers were retired. His nephews and nieces were impressed by the tiger's growth and the smaller ones would roll around on his back. When they got a little rough the cat would give them a cuff and go back to sleep. Lewis always watched him like a hawk. He remembered the man he killed, and wondered if the tiger thought how easy it was to kill a human. The local butcher was always happy to see them and he would give the tiger some meaty bones or an old steak. Lewis always offered to pay him but he would never take the money.

"If you ever wanted to get rid of him I'll take him off your hands."

"You'd probably cut him into steaks, or vice versa." Lewis would kid him.

He would take the tiger and a few friends up into the woods and watch him stalk deer. His friends were always impressed by the lightning speed and quickness of the kill. The Bengal was irritated by loud noise, and after he swatted down one loud motorcycle and shredded a tire, Lewis kept him off the streets. Most of the local cops were vets and gave the complaining biker a ticket. Marie called from

Paris and fed him the latest news on de Beers.

"The Justice department was preparing a case against the company for violation of the antitrust Law, and Congress is asking about their exemption from the commodities market. When they heard about the 'diamonds for Hitler' business they went into orbit. That box was a gold mine; Joseph's deposition and several others were in the box." She continued. "Apparently a black miner was murdered in front of two witnesses and the republic is after Oppenheimer, along with the Belgian government for Joseph's murder. The 'diamonds for Hitler' story was leaked to the press along with a few documents, and is causing a furor. We also heard from the Israelis; they wanted to see the documents from Joseph's box, so we them a package." Marie started laughing, "We also got word that the British Parliament is investigating the London Diamond Exchange. They are digging through the communications between Churchill and Roosevelt during the time when they were trying to do something about the diamond shortage.

Speaking of diamonds," Marie said. "I sent that rock to the best diamond cutter in Amsterdam. He is as closed-mouth as a clam. He checked it out and said that a very large stone could be cut from the large end and a smaller one from the other. What should I tell him?"

"Tell him to go for it." Lewis responded. "I'd love to stick it to de Beers.

DIAMOND / 1959-1961

26

On a spring day on May of '59 Lewis was dozing in his favorite chair on the veranda of his cottage on Sergeants Row at Fort Jackson. It was getting harder for him to keep in shape, and some mornings he was so stiff he could hardly get out of bed. The bullet lodged near his spine caused muscle spasms in his back, and the occasional headache made his eye water. Small pieces of shrapnel would work there way up through his skin. When one surfaced he would pull it out with a pair of pliers. His eye socked leaked and the gunk caused his glass eye to wander, so that most of the time he used his patch over the empty socket.

By 0600 after morning coffee, he took a brisk walk with Hairball and felt better. He had just returned from France, and seeing his young green-eyed son and the happy parents filled him with a longing for a family of his own. *Well, what the Hell* he thought, *I still have my damned cat.*

Marie called as he was checking his calendar for

grandkid birthdays.

"Are you going to be in D.C. anytime soon?"

He hadn't planned on going to the capital, but told her that if it was important he would be there. He left the Bengal at the New Orleans zoo, and arrived at Langley the next day. Three armed CIA agents escorted him to the Company vaults, and Marie met him along with the aging 'keeper' of secrets. He was fingerprinted and when he stepped up for the eye scan he looked at the instrument with his glass eye and set off every alarm in the building.

"Cut the crap, Lewis." Marie snarled, "This is business." The keeper led them to a heavy steel box with a combination lock that Marie opened in seconds. In the box were two diamonds, one huge stone and the other about half the size.

"The man from Amsterdam brought them over in person, with his two sons as guards. The stones cannot be insured as they are priceless," she explained.

"They are beautiful but hardly unique." Lewis said "There are other big diamonds around such as the Hope and the Kohinoor."

"Watch this" she said taking the smaller stone and placing it next to the big one. The diamonds exploded in a kaleidoscope of dazzling colors. Marie held the stones wide apart and the colors faded, and the stones were clear. As she slowly brought them together, a red flash shot from the big stone, and was answered by a blue flash from the smaller one. The intensity and the frequency of the colors

178

increased until they were a few inches apart creating a rainbow of flashing colors. Putting the stones back into the box Marie said,

"They're your rocks Lewis, what are you going to name them?"

"That's easy he replied, The Sisters"

Lewis politely apologized to the elderly keeper for the ruckus with the eye scan. "It broke up another boring day," he replied as they shook hands. They went upstairs to a small conference room where the man from Amsterdam met them. He asked eagerly,

"What did you name them?" When Lewis replied," The Sisters" the little man clapped his hands, and looked at his two sons,.

"I told you so." They sat down at the small table and the 'Clam' got down to business.

"Those stones are old, very very old. They were old when the dinosaurs roamed the earth. Diamonds cannot be carbon dated, but we know they are formed 100 or more miles below the earth's mantle. They are brought to the surface by certain types of volcanoes creating kimberlitic cores. Diamonds found on the surface are one to three billion years old. They are the hardest substance known, but are very brittle. Drop a diamond in a glass of water and it will disappear, remove it and it will be dry. Heat it with a blowtorch, and in a few minutes it will be slightly warm. A diamond will cut through the hardest steel." The Clam paused for a moment. I know diamonds, I love diamonds,

179

but I have no Idea why these stones react to each other so spectacularly. What do you think, Lewis?"

"They just miss each other when they're apart," They mulled this over in silence until one of the sons said, "That's as good an answer as you'll get Pop…Occam's Razor."

"The next big question is what you are going to do with them?" said Marie.

"No Marie, the big question is what Joseph would have done with them, and I will do what Joseph wanted and give them away. Joseph hated de Beers and he passed his legacy on to both of us."

"Not to me, Lewis," she said. "The publicity would ruin me and my career with the Company. And what about you? The man who values his privacy would become a public figure, you and that damned tiger." The Clam raised a calming hand.

"You must have a plan, Lewis, and it's obvious that you have given this a great deal of thought."

"Yes sir, we give the stones to the Smithsonian Institution," he smiled, "with some conditions attached, of course."

They discussed the 'plan' for the rest of the morning. There was some heated discussion on Joseph's memorial plaque, but when Lewis told them that the plaque was his responsibility and not theirs that ended the argument. The next hot topic was money, as none of them had much.

'Filthy lucre' muttered the Clam.

"What about the chips Pop" one of the sons asked, "could you do something with them?" The old mans eyes lit up.

"Maybe I could, it's a real possibility." In answer to Lewis's puzzled look, he explained.

"When you cut up a large stone, some of the waste, or chips, can be used to make smaller stones. If they exhibit the same properties as The Sisters, they would be quite valuable." When he saw Lewis shaking his head, he said,

"De Beers has many enemies, most of them quite wealthy. I can think of two who would rather be dead than sell them to de Beers." They adjourned, each with a piece of the plan.

The first phase or 'chumming for sharks' was Marie's job. She had contacts with two of the board members of the Smithsonian and mentioned to them that she knew someone who possessed one of the largest diamonds in the world, and wanted to donate it to the Institution. The word reached the curator and he called Marie's number at work. She promised him a viewing, but the Company would have to vet him first. The puzzled curator agreed, and in two weeks he was admitted into the vault. Marie went through her act with the stones, and the stunned man left the vault shaking his head.

"Who would give away something like those stones? Second to the Lord's cup, or the Golden Fleece, they would be one of the greatest attractions in the world." The next day the deputy director of the Company asked her what the hell she was working on.

"Just trying to screw de Beers." The old OSS man smiled.

"Nothing personal of course"

The second phase of the plan was in the expert hands of the Clam. Back in his shop in Amsterdam, he managed to cut three small stones from the chips. Two of the stones taken from opposite ends of the rough diamond, acted like ordinary diamonds; But the third smaller stone taken from the chips of the larger stone, and placed with the other two, made them all flash like The Sisters. He called Lewis and told him the story.

"I would like to call my two clients and give them a viewing, and maybe a little history." Lewis told him to go ahead.

Lewis was in charge of the third phase of the plan and it involved going back to the Congo. After another long round trip voyage on the *General Mangin*, he came back with the two witnesses, the murdered miner's widow and all of their families, all agreeing to go to the presentation ceremony. He hoped the Clam could hock the stones for enough to pay all of the expenses, as he had promised the kids a trip to Disneyland.

Two months after they met, they reunited at Langley to share information. Marie told them that the Institutions board of directors was clamoring to view The Sisters. Her boss, the deputy director, had told her that the vault was not a public library, and she could store the stones there, but no more viewers. Lewis was worried about the mounting expense of taking care of the Congolese and their numerous children. Marie, who had access to the Company's 'Black' fund, kept her mouth shut. The Clam said,

"Don't worry about money Lewis. My client offered me two million guilders for the stones, and doubled that after he read Marie's history of de Beers. He hates them as much as I do."

"Why do you hate them so much Pop." Asked one of his sons, and was shocked when he saw tears in his father's eyes. They had been in America when the Germans occupied the Netherlands and had returned home when the war was over.

"The Netherlands was occupied by the SS and not by the Wehrmacht" Your mother and I were part of the *De Geusen*, the Dutch resistance movement. We were captured and your mother sent to the village of Putten, and then sent with the entire village to an extermination camp. I was tortured to name other members, and when I refused I was castrated." The informant was a diamond merchant that worked for de Beers." The young men put their arms around their father, who had doubled over with grief, consoling him with love and tenderness.

Marie and Lewis quietly left the room, and did not speak until they reached the cafeteria.

"Glad I didn't offer to pay him for the work, he probably would have hit me." Lewis said, "But I noticed that you didn't offer anything from your little Black fund."

Marie's eyes went cold, and she said in her mans growling voice.

"I may have to shoot you someday to shut your big mouth." He looked back at her just as coldly.

"Many have tried and failed." he said, then, "I'm sorry kid, I won't mention it again." She bowed her head for a moment, and then looked at Lewis beseechingly

"You are my only family Lewis. I would shoot myself first before I'd ever hurt you."

The next week the Smithsonian board members and the curator waited in the big conference room at Langley. Marie arrived with the steel box accompanied by two armed agents. She showed off the stones again, and the room was filled with gasps of astonishment. She sat the flashing stones on the table so the board members could get a better look. The chairman finally said, pointing at the largest diamond.

"How much does it weigh?" When the Clam told him, he said, "It's probably the largest diamond in the world."

"Perhaps," said the Clam, "but we know little about the British crown jewels or what the Communists took from the czar. But these stones are unique. Nothing I have ever seen compares with the fire from The Sisters."

The chairman offered the curators nuts bronzed to posses the diamonds, and everyone laughed except the curator. Lewis passed copies of the contract around to each board member. It was only two pages and quickly read. A distinguished attorney said it was a pretty simple contract and he could break it in five minutes. Lewis told him to enjoy his last five minutes. Another member was worried about being sued by de Beers. Marie replied that Lewis was giving them the diamonds as he owned them and could prove their provenance. They talked about the cost of the vault and other details. Finally the chairman banged on the table.

"All in favor of accepting the conditions of the contract and the acquisition of The Sisters say aye, all the nays will be shot." The cheering members all shouted their ayes, and the chairman signed the contract.

They tried to keep the gift to the Smithsonian a secret, but too many people knew about the stones and the word leaked out. Soon reporters were sniffing around, and Marie was sent on a 'mission' to France. Work on the viewing room and the vault went on around the clock, and the Institution didn't seem to care about the costs. The Belgian ambassador called Lewis and asked to attend. The Belgians were still angry about Joseph's murder, and wanted to pay their respects to the widow of the murdered miner. Lewis went back to pick up his tiger at the New Orleans zoo, and on to Fort Jackson. The Bengal seemed happy to see him. *H must be all fucked out* Lewis thought sourly, *he probably gets more than I do.* He hid out in his cottage for five months then was called back to DC for the opening.

He hooked up with Marie and they went to the Smithsonian to inspect the viewing room. It was a large spacious room in the Museum of African Art, with a wide entrance and exit. In the center of the room stood a ten foot diameter armored glass vault. On the jet black floor was a circular table covered with black velvet with two robotic white gloved cupped hands. The curator made a motion and the table slowly rotated, the white hands moving slowly together, finally touching for a minute, then moving apart.

"We can adjust the rotation speed of the table, the movement of the hands and the distance apart."

"How do you get in there" Lewis asked. The curator made another motion and the vault rose slowly on its hydraulic lift revealing a small door. A trapdoor opened in the floor and the table stopped rotating. Marie said,

"I suppose the security is good.

"Better than Fort Knox," the curator proudly replied.

The day of the opening the diamonds arrived with armed guards carrying riot guns. The gems were placed in the vault and the table started rotating, and the stones changed from clear to a light show. The demonstration was perfect.

The Congolese families and the Belgian ambassador arrived along with the chairman and the board. After the hands had moved apart and together a few times, a little Congolese girl started crying. Lewis asked her why, in Bantu, and the child said that they were sad when they were apart. Lewis walked over to the curator and told him that the adjustment had to be tweaked a bit and told him why. The hands were adjusted so that when they were apart, the diamonds were clear, but could still flash. Lewis told the child that they could still 'talk,' just like on the telephone.

The Congolese left, with the ambassador insisting on picking up the tab for the visit to Disneyland. In a few minutes the visitors came in, mostly reporters, who had paid the scalpers for a place in front of the line. At the entrance

186

was a large bronze plaque;

IN MEMORY OF JOSEPH VELDT.
MURDERED BY DE BEERS INC.
SERGEANT MAJOR LEWIS SERGEANT
101ST AIRBORNE DIVISION, UNITED STATES ARMY.

Many of the visitors had to be asked gently to move along, as they clung to the guard rail, peering in awe at The Sisters. The curator was amazed by the amount of money in the donation box 'For The Children of Africa' and finally a bit embarrassed. The line never stopped that day, and seemed never to end as the days turned into weeks. The brochures at the exit, gave a history of Joseph, his death, and the OSS report on the diamonds for Hitler. They were widely reprinted causing the worldwide purchase of diamonds to fall dramatically.

Six months later Vinnie called to tell him to watch his back, as there was a price on his head. A day later Marie called with the same news. The bounty was three million dollars. The patrols around his house increased, and the spotlights flashing in his windows kept him awake. He finally told the CO to knock it off, and the lights stopped flashing, but the patrols still crept by. He was getting restless again and called Marie and asked if anything interesting was going on. She said that things were pretty quiet, but she would ask around. She must have done so, as the next day a general from the Pentagon called and asked him if he would like to scout around in Vietnam. "Can I take my cat?" Lewis asked. "No problem," said the general, not knowing that the cat was a full grown Bengal tiger. Lewis received his orders and three months later landed in Saigon.

SHARIA AND CALESTE

27

The Delacroix, twins Sharia and Caleste stood naked facing the huge mirror at the Hotel de Paris. They had never seen a mirror in the first seventeen years of their lives, and five years later were still fascinated by their own image.

"Which one is me and which one is you?" Celeste asked.

"You're Celeste 'cause your jaw is flapping, Sharia giggled." I wonder if old 'limp dick' is still sleeping." They went into the bedroom and looked at the naked body of a man snoring on the huge ornate bed. The body belonged to a very wealthy and famous French swordsman. The twins had whipsawed him. One twin hid while the other moaned and coaxed the man who smiled at his own performance. Celeste excused herself and went to the bathroom. A few minutes later Sharia came out and asked for more of the same. The swordsman obliged, but had to work a bit harder. This went on until the sword was stuck in the scabbard and refused to come out.

"Looks like he's done for the night. Lets go over to the casino and play that wheel game, roll something."

"Roulette you numbskull, lets get dressed."

Marie had taught the twins to behave like proper Parisian women, but it had been a struggle. Their curiosity, beauty and love of life surrounded them like an aurora and attracted men, and some women, like a magnet. Sharia pointed at the rack of chips.

"I'll take some of those pretty blue ones, please."

"I like the red ones, sir." As they waited, chatting with some of the other players, the pit boss returned to the table and asked for their names. When they told him he said that they were not registered, and had no line of credit. Sharia looked at her sister and asked,

"What's Gaston's last name?"

"It's Pin something, Pinhead? She snickered, "It's Pinard, Gaston Pinard."

"I will call Mr. Pinard's room. I need his permission to give you credit for this amount. The twins burst out laughing , and Celeste said,

"You'd better go up and bang on his door. We just fucked his brains out and he's dead to the world."

By the time Gaston arrived, the wheel was surrounded players laughing and shouting, "Which one, which one?" and the twins were pointing to different numbers. He blinked, shook his head and still there were two of them. He, Gaston Pinard, a man of the world, had been hoodwinked by a pair of kids. Sharia saw him first, and lifted her arms to the heavens.

"Lazarus has arisen."

Gaston had the ability, rare among the very wealthy, to laugh at himself. And the twins had given him the best laugh he had in years. So he joined the fun and slammed chips down where ever Sharia picked a number. The wheel of fortune had turned on the casino that night and they lost a weeks profits.

When the twins were ready to go back to their small hotel, Gaston took them aside.

"Half of the money we won belongs to you kids."

"Thank you Gaston, you are a very nice man but Marie told us never to take money or gifts from men."

"Besides Papa wouldn't like it either." Celeste added, "But we could give you something to remember us by if you're up to it." Gaston groaned at the thought.

"I have a weak heart, and it just got weaker thinking about you two in that bed.

The twins dropped into see Marie and Dana. They played with the baby and told them the story about their adventures in Paris. When Gaston Pinard's name was mentioned, Marie's instincts twitched. *That name is familiar, something unpleasant? I'll dig it out later*, but she got caught up in the story and forgot about it.

After Marie finished translating their story. Sharia asked Dana how her job was going at NBC.

"What happened with the interview you were doing on Papa's retirement?" Dana excused herself to change the baby's diaper.

"That's a sore subject with Dana girls. That was the night that Hairball died, and the next day your pappa got the word that his friend Joe Chang was killed. The twins were shocked.

"That's terrible, pappa was very close to Joe. He told us stories about Joe and Sergeant Goat. How did he get killed?"

"I don't know Sharia, Lewis never said anything about it." *But…*

He didn't have to say anything. Lewis and the Bengal disappeared after Joe's family called. The man that had stolen their farm returned with four friends. Joe stood on the veranda and told them to get the hell out. When he turned to go back into the house one of the thief's friends shot him. He was on the veranda dying, and the others shot him to ribbons. Joes family were too afraid to say anything and the police dropped the matter for lack of evidence. But the family did talk to Lewis. The four killers were found in a bar with their throats cut. The thief was a shredded lump of raw meat a few feet away. Lewis had Joe buried in Arlington. He had to collect a few favors but he had a talent for that.

VIETNAM / 1961 to 1977

28

Whenever he went to a different country, Pop studied the culture, the language and the political situation in advance. The more he read the more Vietnam looked like Korea. Both had corrupt dictatorial presidents, and both were divided into North and South. The North was backed by the Communists, and the South by the United States. Each had been ruled for centuries by the Chinese and occupied by the Japanese. Both were very old countries with oral and written histories going back millenniums. Each had been attacked by the Mongols, and only the Vietnamese had defeated them. They both were experts in guerrilla warfare, and in both countries the Communists had infiltrated the Southern governments.

He met with senior agents of the CIA including Marie and the head of station in Vietnam. Lewis told them that he was willing to check out the situation, but it looked like a country to stay out of. The head of station said that if Vietnam went Communist, Laos, Cambodia and Thailand would fall like dominos. Lewis told him the French had lost ninety thousand men in Vietnam, and that the French were good fighters. The French people had definitely been against the war, and if it lasted long, the citizens of the United States would react the same way.

They were an unusual sight walking the streets of Saigon, the huge one-eyed sergeant and the deadly Bengal. When they reached the American embassy the Marines on duty wouldn't let them enter until Lewis showed them his orders. The slick sleeve told him to leave the P-38 at the guard station, but the old sergeant told the kid to shut up. The head of station brought him up to date. There were several hundred Americans in Vietnam and most of them were Special Forces advisors to the Army of the Republic of Vietnam, or ARVN.

"Everyone hates President Diem except the Catholics, but he's still president and we still support him. For all his faults he's the only real political leader in the South, the corrupt old bastard," he muttered. "There is one group of people that hate the North and South Vietnamese equally, and that's the Montagnards. The Vietnamese call them 'Moi' or savages. They live in the highlands, and the name Montagnards in French means Mountain People. The Special Forces guys just call them 'yards".

Lewis asked him if there was a Vietnamese-French speaker around that he could hire to teach him the language. The CIA chief recommended an older man who had fought with the French army. He was one of the few men

194

who had surrendered at Dien Bien Phu and had survived the 500 mile march to prison. "That's because he was one of the two men that escaped."

His name was Louis Paul Boulangerie and said. "Just call me Duex," when Lewis introduced himself. Duex was nearing fifty, had a nose like de Gaulle, innocent blue eyes and almost no teeth.

"Nice pussycat," he said patting the tiger on the head. "I hope he doesn't like French food." They agreed on a salary and Lewis asked him about transportation. There were plenty of old military jeeps in Saigon, and they picked one that hadn't been wrecked by the crazy Vietnamese drivers.

"What's on the agenda, Lewis?" Duex asked,

"I want to check out the Special Forces guys that are training the ARVN and see what kind of soldiers they're turning out." Lewis added, "You'd better get used to being called Duce. They have nicknames for everybody, and it's better than being called Cyclops."

He was wearing his old fatigues with his rank and 101st patch, and the sergeant who was training a platoon, and was hoarse from screaming, welcomed a break. When Lewis asked how it was going, he replied,

"Not worth a shit Top. Their CO is a political hack, and wants a kickback if one of them wants a promotion. We got ten lieutenants that were 'promoted' and we never see them. The godamned army is run by NCOs"

Lewis introduced the Duce, and told the sergeant that Duce had been a sergeant in the French army that had fought the Viet Minh for years before he was captured at Dien Bien Phu. The Duce did not speak English, and when he was asked about the North Vietnamese Army, or NVA, Lewis translated.

"They are very tough and spend lives like water. Their officers are fanatics and men that hesitate in battle are shot immediately. They are expert guerrilla fighters, but when they mass for an attack, they are vulnerable to artillery and aircraft fire."

Sounds like another North Korean army, the Innmum Gun, Lewis thought.

As they were driving out of Saigon Lewis saw some beautiful Eurasian women in the crowded streets.

"Looks like you French have been here a long time," he said. The Duce gave a Gallic shrug.

"Perhaps we will see what American babies look like."

War is hell on kids of mixed races, Lewis thought, *especially the kids with Japanese fathers. He remembered some of the Japanese/Korean orphans that were treated like lepers. Damned Japs, but then he thought of Joe Chang and changed his mind, Joe was American. He remembered some of the Korean mothers selling the services of their daughters so the family could eat. Child whores. What kind of God lets that happen?"*

"What language was that Lewis?"

"Korean, Duce, I was just thinking out loud."

They spent the month at the ARVN training camps. Not many of the company commanders were on the take, and the advisors were pleased at the troop's moral and progress.

One Vietnamese sergeant told Lewis that most of his men were volunteers and hated the Communists.

"The rest are conscripts," he said, "but they're keeping up."

The Duce was astonished at the rate Lewis was learning Vietnamese. He also was getting fond of Hairball. One day Lewis said,

"Let me show you something." The Duce looked up and the Walther appeared as if by magic, pointing between his eyes. He handed it to the startled Duce.

"Its eight rounds are tipped with mercury and sealed. I carry it in a spring loaded, fast draw, holster. It's for your pussycat over there. He killed a man once, ripped his guts out. He was thinking how easy it was to kill a human. He's my friend, but I don't trust him." The Duce looked at the huge Bengal. Somehow he looked strangely different.

Lewis wanted to visit the Montagnards in the Central Highlands where they were being trained as scouts by special forces teams. Since he had to go by a military helicopter, he had to leave the Duce behind.

Lewis paid him a year's salary, and said he would contact him through the American Embassy. Protesting, the Duce said it was too much, and Lewis told him that it was money from a dead Belgian, and to take it.

One of his kids asked Pop where he got his money, and the old man told him it was from his Army pension. Actually he, Marie and the Clam split four million guilders three ways, and Marie held Lewis's share. Some of his women and kids

grumbled a bit about giving The Sisters to the Smithsonian, but Pop went his own way, confident that he would be killed in combat, probably by some kid with a Kalashnikov. Because of Africa and the diamonds he had become famous, and by his own nature, more reclusive. He hated war but knew that it was necessary to combat evil, whether Communism, Fascism, or religious zealotry.

Lewis hitched a ride on a Huey to the Central Highlands to meet Captain John T. Hillman who was working with the Montagnards. He remembered a Hillman from Bastogne when he was a corporal. The captain met him and the cat with a huge grin." Bring that cannon with you?" The Montagnards were ignoring the men and staring at the tiger. They were talking in a dialect that Lewis could not understand. As they walked over to meet the chief, Lewis asked John how he communicated with them.

"High School French mostly, although I have been learning some of their language, he replied. They call themselves Degars, which means 'the people,' I think."

The chief asked about the 'ghost' tiger.' Lewis remembered reading about the Sumatra tigers that once roamed Southeast Asia and were now almost extinct. The tigers that lived in Vietnam, Cambodia and Laos were called Malayan tigers. Lewis explained to the chief that it was a Bengal tiger from India, and that he was born in a zoo. Lewis asked him if he had a goat or pig that he could sell him. The chief said something to a young boy and he ran away, returning with an old male goat. Lewis made soft sound and the cat covered forty feet and killed the goat in an instant. He dragged the goat in back of a tribal long-house to eat (and protect his meal). Lewis offered to pay for the goat but the chief just shook his head. After eating and hiding the remains of the goat, he stretched out in the sun and the children started crawling all over him. *Just like my nieces and nephews* Lewis thought.

He helped Hillman train the 'yards' and rapidly improved his Vietnamese, and from the children he learned the Degar dialect. Walking with the elders, they showed him eatable roots and plants, and the different medicinal plants they used from healing wounds to curing dysentery. Two weeks later they heard the distinctive whopping sound of a Huey, and the 'Snake' dropped in with a load of supplies. He was popular with the children as he always bought them candy.

Lewis admired him for his skill with the Huey, and later in the war, for his incredible courage. He was a small, cheerful man, and had just married a Vietnamese girl. Among the weapons they unloaded were five .50 caliber sniper rifles, with the new Starlight scopes. Lewis had been training his men with the M1 Garand, and was able to pick a team from the best marksmen.

The Montagnards were natural trackers and silent as ghosts. Some of them carried and used ancient crossbows that had been handed down for generations. Lewis had read about the crossbow, and how ineffective it was against the English longbow. But he now saw the advantages of

199

the weapon. It was silent, deadly and accurate for short distance killing.

Hillman taught them how to set Claymore AP mines and how to spot pungi stick traps. When the order came to set up Strategic Hamlets, the chief called the elders and his advisors together to discuss the idea. They all agreed that it was a foolish concept for fighting teams. The chief refused to participate in the plan, which later proved to be unworkable.

Lewis did not trust politicians including President Kennedy. This distrust hardened into contempt after the betrayal of the Cubans at the Bay of Pigs. Lewis believed in the axiom to "Hope for the best and prepare for the worst." With the approval of Hillman and the chief, Lewis and two recon scouts planned a retreat rout to Thailand through Laos in the event that the South lost the war.

Lewis knew that the United States Air Force was building bases in Thailand. He reasoned that the Air Force would help the Montagnards as they were able to rescue downed American airmen. They set out from the village with the tiger leading the way, as his senses were much sharper than any humans. They were able to avoid Pathet Lao patrols, and crossed the Mekong River without incident. In Thailand they contacted the Thai forces and after being disarmed they were escorted to the Royal Air Base of Nakhon Phanom, home of the U.S. Air Rescue and Recovery Team. After the Commander checked out Lewis with the CIA, he listened to the plan to assist the recovery team with Montagnard scouts. The commander knew how vernable the big CH-3 helicopters were to ground fire, and that ground control would be invaluable. They were given radios to communicate with the helicopters and their weapons were returned. A Huey dropped them off at the Thai Laos boarder, as the U.S. still respected the neutrality of Laos in 1962. As they were crossing the Mekong, a Pathet Lao patrol spotted the tiger swimming across the river and started firing. Covering the retreating tiger, the scouts killed several of the patrol, which was quickly reinforced by a company.

My father was very adaptable. He may have been the team leader when dealing with the American brass, but when it came to jungle scouting, he knew his limitations. Chi Rmah without equal in the jungle terrain and they effortlessly switched roles.

Chi and his sister Mia were one quarter French, their maternal grandmother having married to a French soldier. Chi was tall, graceful and rarely spoke. In the years that they were together Lewis, Chi and the Bengal were a formidable fighting team. Chi was the only man that was able to communicate with the cat other than Dad.

Mia was slightly over five feet tall. She was very beautiful and also very strong willed. She was also my mother, and she named me after my uncle Chi.

The team had to travel fifty miles up the Mekong to find an unguarded crossing, but the Pathet Lao patrols hunted them relentlessly. Chi was on point one night and signaled to Lewis to recall the tiger. Chi stood frozen for over an hour, before he started moving again. He had smelled a man that had been smoking. Not the smoke but the faint odor smoke from the mans body.

Beo Ksor, the third member of the team, was renown in the village for the consumption of anything eatable. He was a small thin man who could eat huge quantities and not gain a pound. He also could go for days without eating at all. Beo was deadly with almost any weapon but preferred his crossbow.

The team avoided any platoon size units of Pathet Lao. When they encountered a squad it was annihilated. Bao would move one flank and Chi on the other. When Bao dropped the squad leader, the squad would freeze for an instant and Lewis would turn the tiger loose. He would rip through men tearing and slashing with his claws and disappear. Chi, Bao and Lewis would finish the job with machetes. The squad rarely got off a shot and the team never fired. The Pathet Lao would find the remains of their recon squad, and lose some of their enthusiasm for the hunt.

They finally reached their home in the Highlands. They had been gone six months.

A team of long range scouts spotted a survey team of Viet Cong on the Ho Chi Minh trail and watched them for two days. They were followed by an NVA engineering battalion that was improving the trail for the movement of vehicles and artillery. Hillman reported the activity and the bridges and supply dumps are bombed by ARVN forces. Despite this battalion sized units of NVA forces continue to move south. A company of NVA infantry broke from the trail to hunt and destroy the Degar hamlet. They are destroyed by the waiting Montagnards and the few survivors are tracked down and killed. The NVA did not try again.

In 1963 the Kennedy Administration was growing impatient with President Diem and his conduct of the war against the Viet Cong. Ambassador Henry Cabot Lodge was sent to Vietnam to encourage a coup against the Diem Regime by the Vietnamese military. Ambassador Lodge advocated the removal of Diem and his brother Nhu, but a nervous Kennedy wanted to postpone the coup. It was too late, and Diem and his brother are assassinated. When word reached Lewis in the Highlands, he thought of King Henry II's condemnation of Thomas Becket, *"Will no one rid me of this turbulent priest?"* Like King Henry, Kennedy regretted his words. Although the Diem administration was corrupt, there was no one to take his place among the squabbling generals.

Lewis was depressed by the steady deterioration of the South Vietnamese Army and only his loyalty to the Degar kept him in the country. President Kennedy was assassinated and Johnson became president. Determined not to be the first president to lose a war, Johnson increased the U.S. commitment, and is helped by the Gulf of Tonkin incident.

Chi's sister Mia is encouraged by her family to comfort the depressed American. She was a small, slight beauty, and Lewis immediately responded to her advances. Mia Rmah had the equipment to handle his depression. Although a virgin she quickly became an excellent lover under the sergeant's tutoring. Her muffled cries of pleasure cheered up the men who had grown to love and trust the American. Mia was soon pregnant, and nine months later they became parents of a green-eyed baby boy. Lewis finally had the family he wanted.

All during 1964 the Viet Cong and the NVA continued their buildup in the South. An estimated 170,000 troops faced 23,000 Americans and 100,000 ARVN effectives. The attacks increased against the Americans at Bien Hoa air base, American officers in Saigon, and against the fortified villages around the Capitol. The Degar scouts gave coordinates of Soviet supplied weapons on the Ho Chi Minh trail, which were destroyed by ARVN and American aircraft. The Viet Cong / NVA responded by increasing the anti-aircraft sites along the trail. Three aircraft were shot down by these weapons and two of the pilots rescued by the scouts. The third was killed by the Viet Cong. The two pilots were picked by the Snake at a safe LZ and flown back to Bien Hoa.

The continued infighting of the generals further demoralized the Army of the South, but the importance of the Montagnards increased as the war escalated. Lyndon Johnson was re-elected by a huge majority along with Democrats in the House and Senate.

Lewis called the CIA in Saigon, requesting to be patched through to Marie in D.C. He told Marie that the U.S. was making the same mistakes Vietnam as it did in

Korea, by sending men into Vietnam piecemeal against an overwhelming enemy force. Going into a country where it was impossible to tell friend from foe, was another Korean-style mistake. When Marie asked him what he would do, Lewis replied, "There are three options. Pull out, taking our loyal allies with us including the Montagnards and the Vietnamese that work for us. Or secure strong defensive positions with three or four hundred thousand men and wait for them to mass for an attack. The third thing is to keep the media out of Vietnam. They only show the victims side and not the heroes and they will win the political war for the Communists."

The only reaction to this advice was operation Rolling Thunder, the massive bombing of North Vietnam and the Ho Chi Minh trail. The reaction to the bombing was increased aid to the NVA by the Soviets in the form of Surface to Air Missiles (SAM's). In the three years of bombing over 500 aircraft were shot down, and the Air Rescue Team in Thailand, the 1st Air Calvary in Vietnam and the Montagnard scouts were kept busy. The Snake was fearless, and would fly into the hottest LZ to pick up pilots or the wounded. During the three years of Rolling Thunder he lost four door gunners and had been shot down twice. Captain Hillman put him in twice for the Medal of Honor but his CO did not forward it to Command. The scouts and the Viet Cong got into fierce firefights over downed pilots with the scouts usually winning over the squad-sized searchers of the Viet Cong.

In 1965, on his 47th birthday, the first Republic of Korea (ROK) units arrived in Vietnam. Lewis asked Captain Hillman for permission to visit his friends in the II Corps. When he landed some of the men that he had trained in the 12th Battalion, yelled out 'Wonsa' and ran over to greet him. That evening at the NCO club he met the brother of his old friend Kin Tong-ni, aka Sergeant Goat. Lewis choked up when he saw the younger brother. He had to look away and grab a beer, before he could talk to him. The men gathered around to hear the story of how Sergeant Kim died. Lewis told them in short staccato bursts about the death of the Goat.

"If I had been an instant quicker I could have shot the third man, and I will always regret my failure." They all got mildly drunk and the next day the Wonsa returned to the Highlands.

The Koreans were the cream of the ROK Army, and in their first encounter with the NVA they killed over two hundred of the enemy. In their sweeps of villages for infiltrators or sympathizers the Koreans were brutal in their interrogations. They had learned the hard lessons of Communism and infiltrators were killed on the spot. The Republic of Korea was the largest contributor to the American war effort with over 300,000 men serving in Vietnam on one year rotations. Over 5000 were killed and over 10,000 wounded. They were the first in country in 1965 and the last out in 1973. The NVA was told to avoid the Koreans at all costs unless victory was 100 percent certain. The estimated enemy killed by the ROK army was 41,000.

Australians were fearful of Communist control of Southeast Asia, and joined the U.S. forces in 1962. It was to be the longest war in Australian history, and its involvement ended in 1972. In ten years, over 60,000 men were rotated to Vietnam with 521 killed and 3,000 wounded. Australia entered the war with Prime Minister Menzies and ended with Prime Minister Whitlam.

In the late sixties Lewis and Hillman were busy expanding the Degar scouts and by 1967 they had over two thousand men and their families. The men were trained as experts in different fields. Some specialized in setting Claymore traps: The best marksmen were trained as snipers, while the strongest manned the heavy .50 caliber machineguns. Platoon-sized Rescue Teams were taught to read maps and give coordinates to the Huey's and CH-3s, known as Jolly Green Giants. Others watched the Ho Chi Minh trail and reported the type and number of equipment going south. The best and smartest were the long range scouts that tracked the NVA in and out of Laos and Vietnam. One team traveled to the outskirts of Hanoi and was gone for weeks.

In 1969, a team of scouts tracked an NVA squad with a prisoner back to a hidden compound 35 miles from the Degar camp. They watched the compound for two days and counted six wooden cages and forty guards. The guards worked in two shifts of twenty. While the second shift ate and slept, the first shift guarded the prisoners. The scouts estimated that the cages held 18 to 24 prisoners. What the scouts could not see was a rest camp a few miles away that held two companies of NVA infantry.

Lewis organized his best rescue team along with several specialists, and followed the scouts to the compound. The sergeant carried his special sniper rifle fitted with a vented barrel, silencer and flash guards. They watched the guard's routine for two days and attacked on the second night. Lewis split his team into two parts. The first team would hit the compound where the prisoners were held. The second team would attack the sleeping quarters after the first team secured the prisoners. Chi would lead his six men into the compound after the outside patrols and their dogs, had been silenced.

Lewis was far enough away so the guards would not hear the slight sound of the rifle. The head of first guard on the tower was clear and sharp in the starlight scope. The rifle coughed and the guard dropped without a sound. Chi's scouts crept to the gate of the compound and cracked it open. While Lewis finished off the guard in the second tower, Bao killed the dogs without a sound. The rest of the outside guards were killed by three man scout teams The eight remaining men inside the compound were guarding the cages of the prisoners. The nine scouts in the compound crept behind the cages. Chi nodded and his men rounded the cages in unison and killed the remaining guards. There was a muffled scream from a dying guard that was quickly silenced.

Lewis clicked his radio twice, the signal for the attack on the sleeping quarters. The Degars entered silently each hovering over a bunk like an angel of death. One guard was outside taking a leak. Hearing the thrashes of the dying guards, he peered through a chink in the wall. The terrified man ran towards the rest camp pursued a scout, who lost him in the darkness. The two teams reunited at the compound.

Knowing that they may be followed, Lewis had included the specialists in his retreat plan, and sent the Claymore men ahead to prepare the traps. The prisoners were in bad shape. Beaten, starved with broken bones and jammed into the small cages, they could barely stand let alone walk. The ranking officer, Colonel Chapman, had lost a foot, and had gangrene in the stump. Lewis kicked himself for not bringing stretchers. There were forty of his men for seventeen American officers and one Australian, Captain Boyd. Some of the men had to be tied onto the backs of the scouts, while others could hold on. Lewis took the colonel as he was the heaviest.

"You'd better leave me sergeant. I'm too heavy for your men, and you can't do it alone."

"Shut up and climb on," Lewis snarled, "I haven't got time for heroics." Lewis instructed his men to switch off every mile, and the remaining four scouts to fall behind as a rear guard. As they plodded on Lewis looked for the Claymores and couldn't see them. When he passed his specialist he told him to wait for the following scouts to pass before setting the trip wire. They had traveled three miles when the Claymores went off. Lewis calculated that the NVA were less than an hour behind, and that he'd better slow them down. He jabbed two syrettes of morphine into the colonel's thigh, and leaned him against a tree. He told two of the rear guard scouts to get the colonels legs, one man for each leg, and carry him on their shoulders. He helped them get started, and walking side by side they went up the trail.

Lewis and the other two scouts dropped back a half mile and waited for the enemy. An advance squad of the NVA trotted up the trail and Lewis shot the rear man with the silenced .50. He picked off four more before the others realized they were under fire. Lewis shot the leader and the other two scouts finished off the rest.

When they caught up to the rest of the team, Lewis checked on colonel, who was clear eyed and grinning.

"You'd better give the Aussie a pop, he's in bad shape. Something inside is fucked up." Since all of the team carried morphine, Lewis had one of the scouts give him a 'pop.' He told the two men carrying Chapman that he would take over and they refused, one saying that it was only a leg apiece, the other said,

"It's easy for you, as you've got the lighter side." They laughed, and the Colonel raised a questioning eyebrow. When Lewis translated, Chapman chuckled.

"Black humor at its best." And they started up the trail. As they were still out of radio range, Lewis sent his fastest scout ahead with the radio to give Hillman a situation report and have him send a welcoming committee for the two companies of NVA. The next day they had traveled ten miles with the NVA in hot pursuit. Lewis was starting to get worried, and then he spotted a flicker of movement in the brush, and relaxed. The heavily armed welcoming committee was waiting. Hillman stood and gave him thumbs up. The team continued on. An hour later they heard the sound of heavy gunfire, and six hours later, the Captain showed up with the rest of the team. "We slaughtered them Top. I doubt that two or three escaped." With the help of Hillman's men they made rapid progress. The captain had remembered to bring stretchers, and kidded Lewis about not being prepared. Lewis sulked and told his superior to go fuck himself.

The next day they reached the camp and the two waiting helicopters, a CH-3 and a 1st Cavalry gunship for protection. As usual the Snake was at the controls. *The poor bastards will be well protected* Lewis thought. *If the Snake doesn't get some recognition I'm going to shoot that CO.*

Early in 1968, over 80,000 Viet Cong and NVA launched the Tet offensive against hundreds of towns and cities in South Vietnam. In the fierce fighting, thousands of Viet Cong and NVA troops were killed. They suffer a crushing defeat, and the anticipated popular uprising of the people of the South failed to appear. They lost the battle but won the propaganda war as American support plunged sharply. The American press was almost 100 percent against the war and ignored the systematic executions of 3,000, public officials, officers and Catholic priests in the old imperial city of Hue. Instead they focused on a man suspected of being a Viet Cong guerrilla and shot on television. Hundreds of young Americans fled north to Canada to avoid the draft, and returning servicemen were spat upon and called 'baby killers.' Thousands of protesters around the world wanted the United States out of Vietnam.

My Dad could not believe the abuse heaped on the young servicemen returning to the states from Vietnam. Most of the veterans were the same age as the protesters. How could the men of valor, that fought in World War II, have raised so many pampered brats? The poor and the rural working class served in Vietnam while the elite dodged the draft. When they came into power that same elitist group would send the same young men to fight and die for causes that they deemed important.

His friend and superior, Captain Hillman was promoted to major and given a Silver Star for his work with the Montagnards. Lewis was happy for his well earned promotion and decoration, but despondent when Hillman was reassigned to GHQ in Saigon. He was not replaced, and Lewis was left in charge. The Sergeant was feeling the cold breeze of betrayal on his back and with an almost telepathic sense, his woman and men became uneasy.

Lewis called all his men and their families together and made a short statement.

"Your government may betray you, the United States may betray you, but I will never never betray you. You are my family and my brothers and sisters. We will live or die together."

A week later the Snake dropped into the village with supplies and orders from Command telling him to report to Saigon for reassignment. Lewis asked the Snake to wait for him to send a reply, and he wrote a short letter to Marie and the CIA head of station in Vietnam. The unassuming Snake had opened the orders, not bothering to re-seal them. He grinned at Lewis when he handed him the note and asked why it was smoking. Lewis took him aside and told him,

"Partner, someday we may have to get my people out of here. Those politicians in DC are going to pull the plug and leave us hanging."

"Don't worry Lewis, me and the Jolly Greens will get you guys out." When he flew off Lewis felt a lot better. When Lewis did not report to Saigon, nothing was ever said.

By 1970 the Degars had rescued two hundred airmen, and were awarded the Presidential Citation. The Chief went to Washington to receive the Honor. He innocently asked President Nixon, in French, when their neighbors in Laos, the Hmong were to be equally honored. When the question was translated into English, the President said that was a privilege to honor such a brave people. None of the bored White House reporters understood French, and ignored the translation. They did not know or cared anything about the Hmong. The president, having dodged another bullet about the secret war in Laos, shook hands with the chief and left. Lewis, who had been exchanging information with the Green Berets for years, felt the wind on his back turning into a gale, when his contact, a Green Beret Sergeant, told him of Nixon's refusal to acknowledge the Hmong's help in Laos.

Pop was distracted from the war by the birth of my sister. Mom had a bad delivery and Mister Snake, as I called him, flew in a doctor from Saigon. The doctor said she was anemic and gave her a transfusion. He was correct in his diagnosis and in a few days Mom was chipper as ever. My sister looked so much like my mom that they decided to name her Mia.

The war dragged on. Nixon went to China, and massive worldwide protests against the war continued, amid U.S. troop withdrawals and heavy attacks by the NVA. Nixon's response to the attacks was to order the heavy bombing of North Vietnam and naval gunfire on the NVA massed around the D.M.Z. Peace talks continued, and Nixon went to Russia. General Giap was replaced after the failure of the Tet Offensive in the South.

When the Watergate incident took place, Lewis and his counterparts, the Green Berets, started taking steps to get their people out of Vietnam. The CIA used some of its Black funds to hire freighters and old troop transports and send them to the port city of Chon Buri in the Bight of Bangkok. The Navy, responding to the pressure of naval fliers, sent ships to Thailand. The CH-3 helicopters flew thousands of Hmong, Montagnards and South Vietnamese to the port of Chon Buri. The picture of Jane Fonda sitting on an anti aircraft gun in Hanoi, while men were being tortured under her feet, enraged veterans and many U.S. citizens.

Ships crammed with men, women and children arrive in San Diego, and were refused entry by the Department of Immigration. Threatened by Airmen, Green Berets and the CIA, the department granted political asylum to the refugees. The Watergate affair attracted all the attention of the news media, and the arrival of thousands of Asians in San Diego went almost unnoticed

Back in the Central Highlands, Lewis was having trouble convincing the Chief and over a hundred of his scouts that the Americans were pulling out and they would be killed by the Vietnamese Communists. Mia's family sided with the chief and she refused to leave without her family. Adding to his troubles, the Snake flew in with a stolen ARVN Huey, and told Lewis that the 1st Cav was pulling out and there would be no more drops of supplies and ammo.

The Snake nonchalantly told Lewis that he hadn't enough fuel to get back to base, and planned to park the Huey in the village. He added that he had an envelope for Lewis, that he had not had time to read. Two letters were in the envelope. The first was from the Prime Minister of Australia awarding him the Victoria Cross for the heroic saving of eight Australian airmen. Lewis was starting to get frazzled.

What the hell is that idiot talking about? I remember a Captain Boyd, but not seven other men … but the Hmong picked up seven or eight guys from a Canberra bomber further north. Christ those guys must be home by now, why didn't he just talk to them?

The second letter was from President Nixon telling him to report to the White House to receive the Medal of Honor for the heroic mission to North Vietnam saving the lives of seventy American airmen. A note from Marie was stuck at the bottom. "Wiggle out of that one Hero." The sergeant major went ridged with rage. He may have earned his medal, although he never remembered the action, but he refused to tarnish the honor of men who had earned their countries highest decoration by accepting honors that he did not deserve. He stuffed the letters in his carryall, intending to politely refuse the first and ignore the second botched letter from the President.

Over the years, Lewis had introduced poker into the lives of his family and friends. He had taught them the basics, but after that the Degars made up their own rules. Black cards were bad, especially the black aces. Red cards were good or very good depending on the gender of the player. The women loved the hearts and the men liked the sharp points of the diamonds. Face cards were always good for a family squabble. The king of diamonds was an automatic win for the man, but the queen of hearts beat the king of diamonds if held by a woman. If Lewis held the king and Mia the queen, she would always win by threatening to 'cut him off.' For some unknown reason the CIA had sent the chief a box of krugerrands and the family used them for poker chips. If Mia had a good hand she would giggle and squirm in her seat with eagerness to dump all her coins in the pot. When the game was finished they put them back in the box and shoved it under the stove.

The Degars were unaware that their lookouts had been killed with the same deadly weapons that they had used against the NVA ... the crossbow.

The Viet Cong, emboldened by the absence of most of the scouts, were creeping up on the village. The two companies of hardened veterans expected an easy victory. Lewis would have noticed the tigers flattening ears except he was arguing with Mia. When the Bengal shot out the door, he threw Mia and the children behind the cast iron stove. With the first volley, a ricochet hit Mia in the head killing her instantly.

Lewis saw the light fade from her eyes and went berserk at the sight of his dead wife and terrified children. Grabbing a machete he charged the Viet Cong, joining the Bengal in a killing frenzy. The scouts followed their leader attacking the enemy with knives, guns and even rocks. The big cat was hit in leg and paralyzed by a bullet lodged near his spine. The two companies, frightened by the tiger, the one-eyed giant, and the ferocity of the scouts, broke and ran for their lives.

The scouts had won but they paid dearly for their victory, almost half their number were killed or wounded. Bao was dead and Chi was seriously wounded. The chief was unmarked and the Snake, who was in the thick of the fight, didn't get a scratch.

Pop laid my mother on the bed and calmed me and my

sister. He lay beside Mom's body and stroked her hair. Guarded by Mister Snake with his empty rifle he finally slept. Although physically and emotionally drained, my father did not have time to grieve. He had his wounded men to care for and the suffering tiger had to be put down. As he was preparing to shoot the animal, the old chief put his hand on the weapon, and said that the ghost tigers would save their brother. Dad gave his friend three syrettes of morphine and laid the unconscious animal in the CH-3 with his wounded scouts.

The doctors at the Royal Air Force base in Thailand had to call for reinforcements to care for the influx of wounded men. Finally a sympathetic nurse called one of the surgeons, who was an Animist, to look at the tiger. Lewis told the surgeon that the ghost tigers were caring for the Bengal. The doctor believed, and immediately removed the bullets. The cat had not lost much blood, and rapidly recovered. In some strange way the doctor and the tiger had bonded. They became a familiar sight, the doctor making his rounds and the cat padding silently behind.

In 1973 the Vietnam War ends and all of the remaining American troops are withdrawn from Vietnam. Lewis and other veterans that have fought with the Montagnards in Vietnam and with the Hmong in Laos and Cambodia, continue to work with the CIA, getting thousands of refugees into Thailand. In 1975 the Communists in the North stage a major offensive, and the South falls in less than two months. Lewis sends his children with the Snake and his wife to the safety of the base at Nakhon Phanom in Thailand, while he and the tiger stayed and helped the refugees fleeing the Communists. They had a huge price on their heads, and were easily recognizable. After surviving several ambushes, Lewis decided to leave Vietnam for the safety of Thailand, and in the summer of 1977 they rejoined Snake and the children.

In 1977, facing impeachment for the Watergate cover up, Nixon resigned, and Vice President Gerald Ford became President of the United States. Seeking to rectify the mistakes of his erstwhile boss during the turbulent days of the scandal, President Ford called Lewis to the White House to receive his second Medal of Honor. The day before the Medal ceremony Lewis asked the president for a moment of private conversation. They stepped into the Oval Office followed by two armed and nervous service agents. They weren't about to leave the president alone with the scarfaced giant. The 'moment' took over an hour, while Lewis explained the situation, and why he had to decline the Medal of Honor. He concluded by making his case for his friend the Snake, who had risked his life hundreds of times saving downed pilots. President Ford had served in World War II in the Navy on the carrier USS Monterey. He understood the situation immediately and took steps to rectify the lack of recognition for the Snake's heroism. Two months later Captain William Robert E. Lee Corbet aka Snake was awarded the Medal of Honor amid the cheers of the hundreds of veterans that he had saved. Gerald Ford later recounted that it was the high point in his presidency.

Pop had a lot more problems with the Australians. His polite refusal to accept the Victoria Cross on the grounds that it would dishonor the men that had been killed in far more heroic actions was not acceptable to the Australian prime minister. While agreeing with Lewis that rescuing one prisoner was not worthy of the honor, he told the sergeant that someone had to represent the sacrifice of hundreds of Montagnard lives that were lost saving Australian and American airmen. The PM asked the chairman of the ANZAC association to help convince my father to accept the honor. The chairman refused. The PM bluntly recalled the chairman's war record.

"You were too young for Gallipoli and too old for World War II, and only served in the Home Guard." The Chairman conceded the point, and agreed to talk to Lewis, who adamantly refused. The Australian vets of Vietnam, who were angry at not being allowed to march in the ANZAC day parade, invited Lewis to speak to them in August, the anniversary of their entrance into the Vietnam War in 1962.

He could refuse the prime minister but my father could not refuse the men that he had fought with in three wars. In August of 1978, we arrived in Sydney; Dad, the old chief, us kids and a limping tiger. The prime minister introduced us to the hundreds of veterans that had traveled from all parts of the country to hear their old comrade speak. My father was in his full dress uniform, and addressed the men with unusual eloquence;

"I am not worthy of the honor of joining the membership

of the three Australian men that died in Vietnam fighting the Communists. I can only represent the hundreds of Montegnard and Hmong people that were killed helping Australian and American airmen escape capture and torture. I accept this honor for these valiant people. To you veterans of World War II and Korea, I would say that the men who fought in the unpopular war in Vietnam are worthy of joining your ranks. Thank you."

The Australians who were used to long winded speeches appreciated his brevity and cheered wildly as the prime minister pinned on the decoration. Lewis turned to the old Chief and pinned the Victoria Cross on his chest.

"We shared the war together my brother and this honor belongs to you." The crowed quieted as the old chief started to speak.

"The Communists continue to persecute my people and the Hmong. I ask you generous people to welcome some of them into your country"

Captain Boyd joined them on the platform and thanked Lewis and the scouts that had given him the gift of life. The men of the Canberra bomber that had been rescued by he Hmong gathered around the old Chief and offered to sponsor any of Hmong that wished to immigrate to Australia. This put the Prime Minister in a quandary. The Australia of the seventies had a 'Whites only' policy that barred all Asians from entering the country. They feared the 'yellow hoards' from China and Japan that would make Australia a vassal country of the Southeast. But the Australians made

221

an exception for the Hmong and Montegnards.

It was 1978 and Lewis was almost sixty years old. Marie was two years younger and could have passed as his oldest daughter. The Director of the CIA had wanted to appoint her as Deputy Director, but too many of his department heads were jealous of her accomplishments or afraid of her green-eyed assistant. Lewis went back to his cottage at Fort Jackson, with his ageing tiger. The Bengal was almost twenty five and in tiger years that was a long time.

They were taking their after coffee walk when the tiger broke away from the path and lay down underneath a big oak tree. Lewis sat down with him and for the first time he stroked the tigers head. The animal nuzzled his hand and for the first time in his fierce tiger life he showed affection for his friend. Lewis was deeply touched.

"Cheer up old buddy, he murmured, you've got a few good licks left yet." They stood up and walked home.

SERGEANT SUN TONG ni

29

Lewis had kept in touch with Kim Tong ni's brother after the Korean detachment had left Vietnam. If there was one thing that he regretted in the Korean war it was the death of the Goat. Meeting his friends brother, Sun Tong ni, had been a shock as all of the Goats family had been presumed dead.

After he retired Lewis went back to Korea and spent days with Sun and some of his old friends from the 12th. He found out what had happen to Kim and Suns family. Since Kim was a ROK soldier they killed them. Sun and some of his friends had been in the hills when the Inmim Gun attacked Kaesong. They fought as guerillas, attacking the North Koreans from the rear. When the UN broke out of the Pusan perimeter, they joined the ROK 1 CORPS and the 1st Marine Division in the attack on the Changjin Reservoir.

"Joe Chink really hammered us. We only had cast off

American equipment. We couldn't hold our position and got the blame from the Marines when we broke."

"You did pretty well in Vietnam. The Tuy hoa district was very quiet after your people arrived."

"We learned our lessons the hard way Wonsa. All Marines learn tae kwon do, and we have added a few refinements. We use steel tipped boots and a modified K bar. It's two inches longer and weighs more. We also attacked at night when the Viet Cong were moving into position."

"Sounds like you're ready for some leave time. I want you to meet some friends of mine in Oregon, and on the way we'll drop into DC and see Marie, Dana and the kid."

"I don't take charity Wonsa." Lewis stood up, towering over Sun.

"It won't be charity sergeant," he growled "We'll fly on a military transport to Andrews AFB in DC and stay with my friend Marie. Then hitch a ride to the Air Guard base in Portland. If you're lucky you may get some poon tang."

"How will we get to the United States?" Sun said doubtfully.

"MATs, quit screwing around and get your gear."

"What's poon tang Wonsa?"

Marie and Dana were working and sent the twins to Andrews to pick them up. The twins jumped on Lewis hugging and kissing him. When he finally untangled them he introduced Sergeant Sun Tong ni. Sharia looked him over.

"I heard that Asian men have tiny little dicks," and Celeste added,

224

"And they're quick like rabbits, and flop over when they finish" Lewis translated their comments, verbatim, to Sun who hadn't understood a word of French. Sun smiled at the girls and kissed and bowed over each hand.

"I would be honored to initiate these beautiful women into the ancient arts of the Kama Sutra." Lewis grinned and translated. The twins looked at the sergeant more carefully. He was of average height and broad in the shoulders. His brown face was unmarked, as the scars were on his body, and his large brown eyes regarded the twins with a calm assurance.

"Pappa, when Marie and Dana get back, we'll take Sun out to see what the DC night life has to offer." The's a *noirs* in "Black Broadway" called Ellington's.

"And a Country Western bar called the "Birch" Celeste added.

Lewis gave the twins his, "Don't Fuck With Me" look and said,

"Sun has to be in uniform as he is a member of a foreign military force, and travels on a military passport. Do not, and I repeat, do not get him in trouble. He could get kicked out of the marines if he were arrested in a foreign country. Got that?"

"Yes pappa," they said in unison.

"My God Lewis, you didn't let that poor man go out with those two monsters. The blacks are pretty laid back, but those rednecks at the Birch will kill him."

"I'm not worried about Sun Marie, so relax. *But I am*

worried about the rednecks.

"I wonder if those two will ever get married,"Dana mused. Lewis looked at Marie who nodded slightly.

"They will never get married Dana. One of them, perhaps both, will fall in love but it will never last. They are joined together like Siamese twins, and one would be lost without the other."

"But they love children", Dana said with her eyes misting, "and they told me that they wanted babies."

"They may get them from a sperm bank, but never from a man," Lewis interjected. "The kind of man that they want would never knock them up and walk away. If they both married they would spend too much time apart, and that would never work.

"Tell us your tiger story Dana." Marie said, changing the subject, "I thought I saw some tiny whiskers under the baby's nose." Dana turned red and Marie started laughing.

"I told you that in confidence," Dana said angerly.

"Hell Dana, Lewis was there, he knows more about it than I do."

"But he wasn't on top, Dana muttered.

Celeste called and told Marie not to wait up for them, then hung up. The next day the three of them arrived in a cab, and the twins dropped down on the nearest bed and passed out. Sun was still neat and bright-eyed in his crisp uniform. Sun asked Lewis if he could use one of the showers, and Lewis got him a dry towel.

"Did you have a good time with the girls."

"Oh yes Wonsa, I liked the Birch, It was fun and I met some vets from 'Nam.'

"How did your lessons with the Kama Sutra sit with the girls."

"They are very good students, Wonsa. With practice they will make good disciples.

Lewis called the Snake, who was still in the Air Force National Guard. Robert E Lee Corbet was over fifty but he was probably the best helicopter pilot in the Air Force. He was flying the Long Range HH-60 helicopter for the 939th Rescue Wing out of Portland.

"Lewis, how things hangin'. Where's Chi and little Mia."

"They're staying with the folks Snake. You have anything heading from DC to Portland?"

"I'll call MAC. You may have to layover in Chicago or Denver, but I'll get you home from Portland. The Snake met them in Portland and they climbed aboard the HH60G that was three times larger then the old Huey.

When they flew past the Eugene airport Lewis said.

"Where the hell are you going?"

"You still live in Cottage Grove.?"

"Snake, there's no airfield there."

"Stop fretting, this little bird can land on a nickle and give you some change."

That's one landing I'll never forget. Mr. Snake dropped that bird into a small hole in the trees near our house. The prop wash blew the squirrels out of the trees and every cat and dog within a hundred yards went ass over teakettle. The snake shut her down and asked Pop if his mom had anything to eat.

Over lunch Lewis and Robert E Lee caught up with the military gossip and Lewis translated for Sun, who was being fussed over by missis Sergeant. Chi had heard the noise of the big chopper and had ducked out of school, and little Mia wasn't far behind. Chi hugged his father and shook hands with Sun. He was a very handsome boy with his fathers size and eyes and his mothers grace. Little Mia hugged her father and climbed into the Snakes lap and started talking to him in Vietnamese. Sun looked at the fifteen-year old boy and told Lewis that he was old enough to start taking lessons. Chi answered for his father and said in excellent Korean,

"What kind of lessons honorable friend of my father."

"Tae kwon do" the art of combat, said Sun hiding his astonishment of the boys fluency in Korean.

"He's been working out with his half sister Tong," Lewis explained. "She's home on leave, and giving Chi lessons in Korean and unarmed combat.

"Wonsa, I'm sorry but Korean women do not learn tae kwon do."

"Tong is an American woman, and so is her mother Cindy yu."

Sun has a big surprise coming when he meets Tong. I taught her a lot of tricks but she has a style of her own. Lewis was beginning to regret bringing Sun to Oregon. *I hope the kid survives my fragile little flower.*

Lewis was always amazed by Cindy yu. She was his age

yet her face and figure hadn't changed much in the last forty years. But what really astonished him was the change in his daughter. Tong pored tea for Sun and treated him like royalty. *The downcast eyes and the lilting voice, God almighty, the kid's in love*. Lewis looked at Cindy who smiled and nodded in agreement.

"I believe that you have been teaching young Chi some of the basics of tae kwon do. The five codes of human conduct are important lessons for young men. Have you taught him some of the basic moves?"

"Yes sergeant Sun, Chi is a good student." Sun looked at Lewis,

"With your permission, Wosan, I would like to teach the young man some of basic defense moves of the Marines."

The mat at the high school gym was occupied with young wrestlers, but quickly cleared when the five adults walked in. The Snake had stayed over despite the frantic squawks from the helicopters radio. After seeing Chi's moves, Sun was impressed by the boys grace.

"You move well Chi. Now I'll show how we train recruits in the Marines."

Lewis cringed. He knew how brutal Korean Marine training was and that only a small percentage survived to become part of that elite force.

With a lightning kick he knocked Chi to the mat. When his head cleared Chi attacked and was knocked down again. He was trying to get up when Tong said.

"That's enough." Sun looked into Tong's blazing green

eyes. The 'pussycat' had changed into a tiger.

"You Marines are good at breaking blocks and boards, but why don't you try some of that 'Kung foo' crap on me?" Sun looked at Lewis, who shrugged.

"It's your ass Sun." Suns eyes turned cold and hard,

"I'll kick pretty ass to the moon woman." and swung a kick at her head. A second later he was face down on the mat. When he tried to stand, Tong kicked him in the solar plexus.

"What goes down stays down Sun, rules of combat. You had enough?" Sun was doubled over with pain and could only nod weakly. When he could stand, he looked at Tong with admiration"

"By the belly of Buddha where did you learn to fight like that?"

"Pops taught me most of the moves and I developed a few of my own."

On the way to the house Lewis and the others dropped behind to give Tong and Sun some room to manuvore. Chi remarked,

"My sister sure is a weird duck. First she acts like a damned Geisha, then she almost kills him, now they're chatting like old friends."

"I think it's less like chatting and more like the mating dance of some exotic birds. Cindy laughed,

"Snake you dirty old man, you shouldn't talk that way around children." Chi looked around.

"I don't see any children."

Sun invited Tong out for a night on the town and they drove to Roseburg, and by mutual consent skipped the dancing and went straight to bed.

Korean Marines never quit he thought as he lay beside Tong completely exhausted. Sun had met his match in the sex department.

Tong worked for the State Department as a diplomatic assistant. Bilingual in Korean and English, she also spent several weeks a year in North Korea monitoring their nucular weapons program. Before her next insertion into North Korea, Marie gave Tong very strict instructions.

"Only three people know that you are checking out their Nucular Program. You must never tell anyone what you do or where you go, and that goes double for Sun.

"Why Sun?" He's a decorated Marine,"

"We have no history on him Tong. He wasn't in Kaesong when his family was killed and no record of him or his friends fighting the NKA. All of his family are dead except one old uncle. When we showed the old man a photo of Sun, he did not recognize him.

"Did Pop see him when he visited the Goat's family?"

"No, but Lewis wants to check him out." There is a new path through the DMZ between the American sector and the ROK sector. It's called route 12. A fence panel at the wire has a hidden latch and only the Company knows the code key. I will dummy up a message with the date of your departure, the route 12 location and the code key. When you go back to Korea you'll be seeing Sun again. When he has the information he will want to check it out.

"How will I get this information to Sun?" Tong was dazed by conflicting emotions. *Not Sun he's a good man and a wonderful lover, but if Pops wants to check him out, we'll check him out.*

"It will be in your purse. On your next date go to the powder room and leave your purse with Sun. If he's clean we'll know it."

"How will you know?"

"White bond paper takes excellent fingerprints, Marie said dryly."

The black figure ghosted up the trail to the fence and touched the panel that seperated the two Koreas. The small, almost invisable code disks were difficult to see through the small slits in the black mask. He entered the code

and with a slight click the panel opened. As he stepped through the fence into North Korea, he was riddled by automatic weapon fire. Captain Kim Jong su of the State Security Department of North Korea was dead.

Lewis and Tong listened to the staccato burst of gunfire coming from the line where thousands of Koreans were killed trying to escape the brutality of Communism. Tong hugged her father as tears coursed down her face.

"Daddy, why did he want to kill me? I thought he loved me." Lewis stroked her silky black hair.

"When he was fighting Chi, were you watching his eyes?"

"No I was watching Chi."

"When you yelled' That's Enough" you were angry, why?"

Tong thought a moment

"Because … because he seemed to be enjoying kicking he hell out of a kid."

"That's what I thought too, honey. Marie had him checked out through the KCIA and it seems that his life started when the ROK 1st Corps was retreating from the Chandjin Reservoir. They would have interrogated him except for his exceptional valor in Vietnam. Tong wiped her eyes and sighed,

"Why didn't they just grab him? All they would have to do is rip that mask off and see that it wasn't me. Lewis hugged his daughter and buried his face in her hair. "It wasn't the North Koreans that killed him," he whispered, "It was the KCIA. Tong you have diplomatic immunity. Alive you're an embarrassment. Dead and buried you just disappeared, another causality of the cold war."

"Problem is Pop I think I'm pregnant."

DISCHARGE / 1978

30

"Sergeant Lewis, why did you pick me out of all those other media anchors with a lot bigger following than mine?" Dana asked. She was a sexy woman from the media pool that Lewis had grudgingly allowed to cover his retirement. The Vietnam War coverage had turned his disgust of the media into outright loathing.

"Because you are the brat of a good friend of mine" Lewis replied. *She was Vincent Shapiro's daughter, and probably a hell raiser like her father*, he thought.

"You have been through three wars, have more decorations than God and have never given an interview in your life, so why now? "Lewis reflected on this for a moment, and decided to be diplomatic.

"Army regulations require that all questions of a strategic or tactical nature be answered by a public information officer. Until Sunday I am still a sergeant. Monday I will be a civilian, and will be able to answer most of your questions."

"How about a few background questions and a two day tour of your unit while you are still a sergeant major," she persisted. "I will promise for myself and Dave that we won't use anything until after the interview is complete"

"Okay. Lewis replied, "Fire away."

They set up on the front porch of Lewis's small cottage on Sergeants Row. Lewis sat on a worn, comfortable armchair, smoking a cigar and sipping at a bottle of Nippon Three Star, with the big cat dozing at his side.

"Look at the red light," Dave said to Lewis, and to Dana, "Roll it"

"This is Dana Shapiro at Fort Campbell, Kentucky home of the 101st Airborne Division, with an exclusive interview with Sergeant Major Lewis Sergeant who will retire after over 40 years of service with the United States Army. Sergeant, my first question is why does the Military let you keep a tiger on this base?'

"Well Dana" Lewis replied, "my furry friend is a mascot, and he is also a weapon. He has killed more Viet Cong than you or I could count. The Montagnards love him and used to leave tiger patches on his victims. He can hear or smell an enemy sooner than any human and can attack in complete silence. He scared the hell out of the Viet Cong, and a tiger patch on a trail would stop an enemy force in its tracks. He can also spot booby traps, such as captured Claymores and Pungi sticks, and he usually marks them."

"How?" she asked.

"He pisses on them." Dave gave the 'beep' sign.

"How do you control him?"

"I mostly don't. He is his own master when he is in his own environment."

"You were one of the first 'advisors' in Vietnam and the last one out. In fact you declined the Medal of Honor, had an exchange of words with the President, and returned to Vietnam for almost two years. What happened?"

"No comment until Monday, and its time for my rounds." They walked to the parade ground where the flag was being lowered for the night. *The haunting sound of Taps,* Lewis thought, *how many souls had that sound sent into the void?* His eye misted over. *Christ, he gritted, why don't you just cry for the damn camera. Suck it up you old fool.* Lewis looked at his watch.

"I have to go, so be at my place at 0600." Dana turned to here cameraman.

"Dave why don't you go back to the guest quarters, and let me have a few words in private with the sergeant." She turned to Lewis "If that is okay with you?" Lewis gave her a long thoughtful look. *She was a beautiful, talented woman and she would probably fuck a dying leper to get a story. She will try to seduce me into telling all because of the so called public right to know. She's done her research and knows about Marie, so I'll let Marie handle her.*

They returned to the cottage, where Lewis put two steaks on the grill and fed four raw ones to the Tiger. Lewis was getting strange but familiar vibrations from Dana. As they were eating their steaks, she started asking him

237

questions about his personal life, why had he never married, how many children had he fathered, and finally, blushingly, if he was hung like rumor had it.

I had to get this story out of Marie as Dana would never say anything. Dana was a very noisy lover with some interesting sound effects. These particular sounds attracted the attention of old Hairball, and the next thing Dana felt was the soft belly fur of a tiger on her back, and tiger spit dripping off her tits. I never found out what happened after that. Marie would laugh, then sit with that thousand yard stare. She was family, and I never asked so I filled in the blanks.

Lewis looked up over her shoulder and saw the head of the great tiger. Dana felt the soft fur of the tigers belly on her back, and saw the huge clawed paw next to her hand. The massive jaws closed on her neck and hot saliva ran down her neck and onto her breasts. She looked at Lewis, terrified.

"Don't move," he said. He gave a soft snort and the cat let go of Dana's neck and padded over to his rug and laid down. Dana lay on Lewis, her body shaking with fear and a feeling of having survived a brush with death.

"Why did he do that?" she finally croaked.

"Because you make a noise like a female tiger in heat and he was checking you out."

"What would have happened if I hadn't checked out?"

"Your head would probably be in my lap." Lewis smiled to himself and thought, *good for you old friend, you just scared the shit out of a reporter.*

After Dana had left, Lewis stripped, took a shower, and checked the doors and windows. He looked at the tiger and saw that he wasn't breathing. He sat down and stroked the cats head, and thought of all the years they had together.

He felt a pain in his heart greater than the lost loves of his many women. A mans love for a comrade is different that his love for a woman. He remembered the apologetic look of the dying Goat, the tiger nuzzling his hand affectionately, and the stark white cross over Joe's grave at Arlington. And for the first time in his life he bowed his head and wept.

Saturday they continued their tour and filmed the sergeant major at work. As they walked along officers, including one general saluted Lewis who returned their salutes.

"Why do they salute you first? "I thought the lesser ranks saluted first?" Dave asked.

"They are paying homage to Danas beauty" Dana poked him,

"They salute the medal not the man" They toured the rifle range, and Lewis corrected some of the men. He took special interest in the advanced unarmed combat course that included Special Forces and CIA men and women.

One lithe Asian woman came in fast and hard, and at the last moment launched a flying kick at the instructor's padded chest, knocking him down.

"Don't ever leave your feet" Lewis yelled, "You are wide open to a counter strike" The Asian smiled at him.

"Care to try me Pops?" Lewis smiled back at her, and walked onto the mat. The instructor groaned,

"Better call the medics" Quick as a cat she flew at him looking into his eye, and at the last moment aimed a two footed kick at his knees. Lewis kicked her legs aside and dropped a knee, stopping an inch from her chest. "You're dead" he said, and for an hour he worked with her. She tried a stiff hand shot at his eye; Lewis ducked, got inside her guard, and cracked her on the jaw with his elbow. She countered with a knee to the groin and Lewis blocked it with his hip, and hit her under the nose with the heel of his hand. All the while, Lewis explained his moves to the group.

"Use all parts of the body, an elbow to the jaw can incapacitate but an elbow to the neck can kill. The heel of the hand under the nose will drive the nasal bone into the brain for a quick silent kill." He helped the bloody sweating Asian woman to her feet, and looked into her fierce green eyes.

"You are a good student, fast smart and courageous." She bowed to him.

"Thank you for the lesson father."

"Your enemies will fear you, my daughter"

That night Dana stayed with Lewis, making love and talking. Her hand traveled over the scars on his body. *You have shed a lot of blood for your country old man,* she thought.

Sunday morning Fox Company of the 101st Airborne Division passed in review then halted at the bleachers that were filled to capacity to honor the nation's most famous soldier. The Commanding General of Fort Jackson said a few words;

"I was a green second lieutenant in Fox Company when we surrounded a stone farmhouse that was being defended by a squad of SS Storm Troupers. The sergeant told them to surrender or we would roast them with a flamethrower. They walked out the door yelling "Kamrad"; I stood up and ordered my men to secure the prisoners. Sergeant Lewis pulled out his pistol and shot the first two men in the head. The first man had a light machinegun strapped to his back. I can still recall the sergeant's words of advice. "Grow up or die dipshit". The solemn occasion was broken up by hoots of laughter from Fox Company and the crowd in the bleachers. The general continued,

"I will now turn this ceremony over to my friend and mentor, Sergeant Major Lewis Sergeant."

When the noise had died down, Lewis nodded to the general and said,

"Men I would like to leave you with one word of advice. Always carry dry socks." With those words Sergeant Major Lewis Sergeant ended his forty year military career.

The following day, Dana continued with her interview.

"Sergeant, excuse me, "she smiled. "Mister, Sergeant. "What are your plans for the future? You had some words with President Ford when he was going to present you with your second Medal of Honor, which you refused." Lewis was silent for so long that Dana was beginning to think he wasn't going to answer.

"President Ford is a good man," he said, "I was angry at

my country's treatment of the Hmong and the Montagnard people who fought along side of us and saved hundreds of lives. Why should I get a medal for the rescue of seventeen POWs when it was forty-five Montagnards that helped kill the guards and carried the prisoners thirty-five miles to the nearest LZ."

"But you got thousands of them out of Vietnam," she interjected.

"Sure "he said bitterly, And most of them are in Australia or in camps in Thailand. And what about the Snake who met us at the LZ and ferried those POWs out? That medal belonged to the him and President Ford had the guts to give it to him."

Dana figured she had better save the hard stuff, as Lewis was getting angry and might say something that would be cut.

"You grew up in logging country, and lost your uncles in World War I. What to you remember the most about your family?"

"I have a great family Dana. My they're very patriotic, and my brothers had a fit when I went into the army, and they couldn't pass the physical. My oldest brother kissed a choker and was rejected for false teeth. Tom, the youngest, had a heart murmur that he claimed was gas, but he was rejected by the Army, Navy, and Marines. My dad told him to put on a wig and try for the WACs. He didn't talk to pop for a month."

"You were a lumberjack also?

"Logger, not lumberjack." he said. "I worked on the rigging, and at times it was more dangerous than combat. Tom was a cutter or faller, and some of those big Doug fir were ten feet across at the stump. When they smashed through the smaller timber the chunks came down like rain. They rejected him for his heart, but if they had x-rayed him and found that his back had been broken in three places, he would have been bounced anyway."

"What happened to his back?"

"Barber chair," And seeing Dana's blank look he explained "It's when you are cutting a tree, and it splits up the middle and swings on top of the split, like a capital T. A big one can reach 40 feet behind you, and when it drops it could fall on either side. His partner ran and Tom tried to save their saw. He waited too long and got clipped.

Dana could see what Lewis was trying to do. He would much rather talk about things other than himself. Time to drag him back to a few political hot spots.

"How do you feel about homosexuals in the military?"

"No problem Dana, a faggot has as much courage as anyone else, and they have a right to serve their country. Those Nazi bastards killed them off as undesirables along with Jews, Jehovah witnesses, Gypsy's, Slavs and other so called sub-humans"

"What about Negroes. Don't they have the same right to serve their country, but they didn't get the chance in World War II."

"Get your facts straight, Dana. Ike integrated the military

243

and I fought along-side the 969th Field Artillery at Bastogne, and they were 'Negroes'. Blacks in Korea were just as good as some of the southern boys that hated them. Funny thing though, we fought along side of a company of coal-black Ethiopians in Korea that were probably the best night fighters in the world, and the southern boys admired them. Women have the same rights, and someday we will see them in combat roles. Lewis the prophet has spoken." he said with a grin.

"Lewis, as far as name recognition, more people know and respect you than any other person in the country. Have you ever considered going into politics and run for president?" Lewis choked on his cigar. When he finally stopped coughing, he wheezed,

"You have got to be kidding. First I value my privacy and that is the first thing you lose. Second, I do not want any part of the political scene. And last, I am not electable."

"But...

"You're going to ask why, and I'll tell you, by the numbers. First, in the next few years, the Soviet Union will fall apart. When this happens I would withdraw all American forces from Europe, including nuclear weapons; Two, I would pass a flat tax of fifteen percent on every adult in the U.S., junk the present tax system and cut the IRS in half; Three, I would get Congress to pass a Term Limits bill, eight years for the House and the same for the Senate. If they refused I would get two-thirds of the States on my side and amend the Constitution; Four, I would require a means test for Social Security; Five, I would resurrect the draft, and require everyone eighteen and older to join the military, or the Peace Corps; Six, I would pay my service men and women a living wage so they would not be forced to live on food stamps; Seven, I would pass a tort reform bill limiting punitive damages on doctors and hospitals and eliminate federal education money to Law schools; Eight, I would legalize Pot and tax it; There are several other things that I'd do but I think that this would be enough to put me out of contention."

Dana stared at him with her mouth open, until she noticed Dave pointing the camera at her, and snapped it shut.

"Before we take a break Lewis, tell me if you had been the president during the Vietnam War, how would you have handled Jane Fonda's visit to Hanoi?

"That's easy Dana. I would have her tried for treason and shot".

So much for a presidential candidate, Dana thought sourly, her dreams of being a king maker fading.

That night Dana sat in her room mulling over her notes. *Forty years in the military and fast approaching sixty,* she thought, *and he can still fight and fuck real good and I should know.* She smiled to herself. *You don't get to be a news anchor with NBC by being a virgin. I know his history and his body but I don't know the man and what makes him tick. I'll need to do some serious research and talk to some of his friends and or lovers. This is going to be a long and expensive project, and I'll need some serious backing. I'll talk to that hermaphrodite that just retired from the CIA. That should stir things up.* She spent two more days with Lewis, and then packed up, leaving him with the impression that the story would be a short clip after the evening news.

Back in New York, Dana started maneuvering to get the backing for her story. She showed her editor clips of Lewis's eight point political policies and the fight between him and his daughter.

"You have got to be kidding Dana. You mean that pretty asian woman is his daughter?"

"Boss, I just found out about that when I got the English translation."

"That's good work Dana and those eight points are a real bombshell. It's a great story so why don't we just run it right now?"

"It's a good story now, but with a lot of work it will get us top ratings. This woman, Marie Vasquez, just retired as head of station of the CIA in France." Dana continued, "She and Lewis worked together during World War II and may have been lovers, and that could make the bombshell into a fizzle by comparison." The editor thought a minute… *Young, ambitious reporters come and go but expenses are forever,* teetering, then said, "Go for it."

With her editor clearing the way, Dana spoke to the deputy director of the CIA. She told him that she was doing a story on the life of Lewis Sergeant, and asked if the CIA would have any objection to an interview with Marie Vasquez about her work with Lewis in World War II. The

DD hesitated a moment and said,

"Just about World War II?" Dana was puzzled but said,

"Yes just about the war that Ms Vasquez and Lewis were in together."

"No problem" said the DD. "I'll call up Marie and set up an appointment. She lives in France you know." Dana called Air France and bought two tickets to Paris.

When Dana first saw Marie Vasquez she was shocked. The woman was beautiful. She was over fifty but could pass as a woman in her early forties. She ushered them into her apartment and told Dave to set up his equipment anywhere he liked. The women chatted while Dave fussed with his cameras. Dana was captivated, and discovered that she really liked Marie Vasquez. After the introductions, Dana started the interview with her stock in trade; the hard ball.

"Marie, were you and Lewis lovers?" Marie gave her a cool look and said,

"No dear, Lewis is a man and I am a man in a woman's body. We both love women and I find you much more attractive than Lewis." *Wow* Dana thought with a little twitch in her groin, *the plot thickens.*

"You know Lewis as a soldier and a friend, what is he really like?" Marie thought for a moment,

"Lewis is quite good at killing people, but he takes no pleasure in it. Back then, I on the other hand, would have rather killed a German than made love to a French woman. I think Lewis thought I was a barbarian, but he never said anything."

Marie paused, she was watching Dave who had bumped into an end table with a small ivory horse that was grazing on a green velvet cloth. Dana blinked, the little horse had moved, she shook her head and looked again. Yup it's just an ivory horse. Dana caught up with Marie. On the way to Bastogne, I killed an American captain that wanted our car to escape the Germans. Lewis stuck the Captains' gun in the knife wound and blew his head off so it would look like suicide. Lewis gave the car to some wounded soldiers. It was Bill Donovan's car and I think Bill was a bit miffed about it."

Marie talked about their experiences in the fighting around Bastogne and her love of the 101st Airborne.

"I received the Legion of Honor from president de Gaulle but the men of the 101st made me an honorary member of the Screaming Eagles. I treasure that patch more than the medal."

It was getting dark and Marie insisted that Dana and Dave stay in her apartment rather than a hotel. "I have plenty of room" she said, and after a light supper, led them to their bedrooms. Dana reviewed the notes on the questions she would ask Marie in the morning. Then, feeling restless, she stole downstairs to get a glass of water from the kitchen. When she turned, glass in hand, she saw Marie standing there, lowering a silenced pistol, the cold light of indifference fading from her eyes.

"Forgive me Dana, I'm a light sleeper, too many years with the Company, I'm afraid."

Danas' hand started to shake. Now she knew why Marie was watching Dave and thanked God that the little horse wasn't damaged. Marie quickly went to her, and wrapping her arm around her, led her to a couch. Marie stroked her hair gently until she stopped shaking, and then softly kissed her on the lips. Gratefully Dana returned the kiss and soon they were taking off their clothes, kissing and stroking each other.

"God, Marie" Dana said, "I never thought I'd be making love to a woman but with you it feels right." Then she fondled Marie's dying erection.

"That thing pretty well kills my theory of you and Lewis being lovers." She looked at Marie, grinned and added, "But you ruined the best part of my story."

The following day, Dave went on a sightseeing tour, and Marie and Dana stayed at the apartment talking and making love.

"Marie," Dana asked, "did Lewis ever do anything for the CIA?" Marie looked at her and replied in her man's voice,

"Don't ask, you may get hurt."

"You have never used that voice before" Dana said, "It's scary and why now?"

"Because I'm serious and probably falling in love with you. There are things about the work that Lewis did in Vietnam that are very classified,"

God, the kid is just like Vinnie, smart, devious, innocent very perceptive and wrapped in a body that won't quit. "Look Dana, the CIA s first mission is to protect itself and collecting intelligence and spying is a distant second. They would

249

never use 'extreme prejudice' on a US citizen. That would be illegal, but believe me, my dear, they could and will cut you off at the knees if they feel that you are a threat, and you would never know it."

"Thanks Marie," Dana said with tears in her eyes, "I love you too, girl. You're quite a man. And my lips are sealed about Vietnam."

Back in New York, Dana sat with her editor reviewing the footage of the interview with Marie.

"What do you think about Marie? Her editor asked. "That business of her killing an American captain and Lewis blowing his head off sounds pretty farfetched."

"Boss you saw the tapes, the woman is gorgeous, but you didn't see the look in her eyes when I mentioned the CIA. It was the look of a stone killer."

"That part about the CIA wasn't on the tapes, Dana, you didn't fool around a bit to get the story, did you?" her boss said gently. Dana colored slightly,

"Well, not much."

The next day Dana called Fort Campbell and learned that Lewis had left for Oregon to visit his family. When she called his home, his mother said he was hunting elk with his brothers. *How the hell he can get around so fast lugging that damned tiger*, not knowing the animal was dead. She desperately wanted to talk to him about Marie, so she caught the next plane to Oregon. Everyone in Cottage Grove knew where he Sergeants lived, and the taxi from the Eugene airport had no trouble finding the large old house that was shaded by two huge maple trees.

Misses Sergeant hugged her at the door, got her to the kitchen, and plied her with cookies and lemonade. She was over eighty, but sharp as a tack.

"He bedded you' didn't he? I can always tell. I have grandchildren I know about and more I don't know about. If you're pregnant, I hope it's a girl, and she'll be a beauty if she looks like her mother." Dana smiled at the old lady, and confided that Lewis didn't get her pregnant and that they were just very good fiends.

The men came in the house with a bloody elk liver for dinner, interrupting the inquisition. The brothers joked and kidded with Dena, then left for their own homes and families. The boys called their mother 'Top,' or 'Top Kick,' the nickname for a sergeant major. Over dinner Dana asked Lewis about the absence of his tiger. Lewis and told her that he was visiting his girlfriends at the Portland zoo.

"He likes making baby tigers," he explained. The Top glared at him.

"Lewis, don't talk like that in the presence of a young lady and your mother."

"Sorry Mom, sorry Dana," said the country's most famous killer.

When the old lady went to bed, they grabbed some beer and retired to the swing on the front porch. Lewis was smoking a cigar with his feet comfortably on the rail, while Dana was twitching on the seat beside him. Finally Lewis said,

"What's wrong, kid?" and Dana blurted out,

"Lewis, I'm in love with Marie and I don't know what to do. I'm the top anchor at NBC and I don't want to give that up, but I want Marie, and I want a family."

Lewis stared at the smoke curling from his cigar. What can I say, he thought, *the truth, like the CIA says, will make you free.*

"Well Dana I'll tell you a story my dad told me. Once there was a king that had just sentenced a thief to be hanged. The thief said to the king, 'Give me one year and I will teach your horse to sing.' The king agreed and the thief went out to the stables and started singing to the horse. The kings' stable master laughed at the thief and told him he would never get the horse to sing. The thief shrugged and said philosophically, 'In a year the king may die or I may die, or perhaps the horse will learn to sing.' In other words you have the time to resolve this problem.

The first thing you should do is go back to Paris and talk to Marie. She is a very wise woman, and if she loves you like you love her, then you will find a solution."

"Thank you Lewis" Dana said, and then added with a smile, "Want to have a last fling before I walk down the aisle?" Lewis was shocked.

"In my mothers' house? You've got to be kidding."

"I am," she replied, and they went to their separate rooms.

Dana called Marie the next day from New York.

"Marie, I have got to see you. When could I come to Paris?"

"Don't bother Dana; I have to go to DC on business. I'll call you when I get to New York." When Dana picked Marie up at the airport, they hugged like old friends, but inside Dana's car they exchanged passionate kisses and gropes.

Driving to Dana's apartment, Dana told her the whole story, even Lewis's king and horse fable.

"Lewis gave you some pretty good advice, especially about how problems sometimes solve themselves over time, lover, but I think that this one will be solved in a few days. As they pulled up to Dana's apartment, she gave Marie a happy smile and said,

"Tell me."

"Later kiddo, you'll have to work for it." After an exhausting session they sat in the kitchen sipping hot tea.

"It looks like the Company is going to offer me a job." Marie said, "I think it's undercover, and not under the covers with you either," she added. "The only things I know is that I would be stationed in Washington, and they want to ask me some questions about the Lewis interview."

"What kind of questions?" Dana said, looking worried.

"If its undercover work they'll ask you to do the interview over in a blank room, with my face in a shadow. If you refuse they will probably withdraw the job offer."

We'll see if this is love or lust Marie thought, looking at Dana wistfully. "No problem," if they want to scrub the whole I would be very disappointed, because it's very good, but if you'll be going undercover it would be very dangerous and I would never do that to you." Two days after

253

arriving in Washington, Marie called Dana at work and said that said that the CIA wanted her to work in intelligence and not operations.

Well that was the last of Dana's story on Pop's life. She and Marie were married. Vinnie gave the bride away and Dad was best man. Dana got knocked up, probably on their wedding night, as the kid was born nine months from the day of the wedding. She liked being a mother and when she got pregnant again, she gave up her job with NBC. I was assigned to Covert Ops and sent to the Russian language school at the Presidio. I inherited Pop's gift for languages, and can speak Russian like a native. When I finished language school I reported back to Marie at Langley. She looked tired, and told me that I had better start looking for another job as some very powerful people in Washington wanted her gone. The Director was retiring and these people wanted her out of contention for the job. She smiled wanly, "Must still be a few Hermaphrophobes left in the old boy Congress."

Dad was visiting Cindy Chu and my half sister Tong Chu in Eugene. Weird name for a fox like her, but like most of us kids there was a history behind it. When Cindy wrote my Dad, he was in Korea training recruits. There was a wiseass kid he liked named Kim Tong ni. When she told him that she was pregnant, he told her that if it was a boy to name him Kim. Her parents told her Kim Chu sounded too much like Kimchi, a Korean dish made of cabbage, fermented fish heads, rice and leftovers. When a baby girl popped out, Cindy named her Tong Chu. Pop got sucked up in the Korean War and by the time he got out of the hospital, Cindy had married a fat little history professor. Tong loved my dad and he showed her every dirty move in the world of unarmed combat. She got knocked up by a North Koran Marine, but it seemed to make her tougher. In the world of martial arts Tong had no equal.

I filled the old man in on Marie's problem. He was quiet for so long that I was about to repeat myself, when he said that he would look into it, and he did.

Lewis was always examining things that happened years ago, and did not always pay attention to what was happening in the present. When he came home from Vietnam with a ten year old boy and a baby girl, he was an emotional cripple. Marie had taken charge of his life and the lives of the kids… they were the family she never had. She was there for him and he would be there for her, and the thought of his best friend in trouble sharpened his mind like a razor. The powerful men that were trying to destroy her smelled to him like corruption, manipulation and money. Diamond money. Marie and Lewis had exposed de Beers and those megalomaniacs needed to destroy Marie. She knew where all the bodies were buried. Lewis called a few friends and picked up the floor plans for the Watergate hotel.

Senator P. Jon Smithe was a Rhodes Scholar and senior

member of the Committee of Jurisdiction. He smiled when he learned that President Carter was leaning towards Marie Vasquez as Director of the CIA. His contacts at Oxford had made him a rich and powerful man. Now he was in a position to repay the Company that had done so much to make him a United States Senator. He had already started a program of character assassination, and was preparing a leak to the media that Marie had been in charge of Project Phoenix in Vietnam. The Senator was working on the questions that he would ask Marie at the first committee hearing, when he felt a slight breeze on his back. Turning around, he looked into the terrifying evil eye, and the scarred face Lewis Sergeant.

"Writing your last words Senator?" Lewis asked.

He leaned over and looked at the notes.

"Good guess Senator. Marie was running the Phoenix operation. She used me for special jobs, like long range stuff." He reached up and raised the Senators upper lip with his finger. "I could hit that little sparkle of gold with my big .50, from a mile away, and blow it clean out of your mouth, with a chunk of your head along with it of course."

Smithe felt the hot urine pooling in his pants, and his gut wrenching fear was starting to loosen his bowels. The evil eye had worked its magic.

"How did you get in here," he finally squeaked, "and what do you want from me?"

Lewis stood up, and the Senator noticed he was casually dressed, and not wearing some kind of black Ninja suit,

"Ever heard of the Shadow Team?" he said. "They get people like me into places like this to explain things to people like you. We know about the favors that you did for the diamond industry, and how you amassed a fortune selling quality stones that were given to you as 'campaign contributions.' If you thought that your activities were untraceable better think again. Unpaid income is not tax free and you could be looking at hard time. We want just two things from you. First your enthusiastic support for Ms Vasquez as director of the CIA, and second your resignation from the Senate. If you don't agree to these conditions, your activities could be leaked to the press. You may become despondent, even suicidal and maybe even jump from this same eleventh floor apartment. Your Trophy wife would grieve for about ten minutes, and then marry your young chief of staff that she's been fucking. Agree and you can enjoy your retirement in comfort, secure in the knowledge that you did the honorable thing. Have a pleasant evening, Senator." And Lewis walked from the room. Smithe sat rooted in his chair, his thoughts rabbiting around in his brain; *He can't do anything to a United States Senator. God I'd better hide those stones… George wouldn't do that to me with Muffy. I'll kill them both the rotten traitors. Calm, be calm you can think your way out of this. He wasn't threatening me, he wasn't angry, just giving instructions… indifferent. Then why is shit running down my leg?*

President Carter chose Marie Vasquez for Director of the CIA, and her confirmation was unopposed in the

Senate. Ex Senator Smithe did not live long enough to enjoy his wealth. The diamond industry was not happy with his enthusiastic support of the new director and he fell to his death from his eleventh floor balcony.

As Director of the CIA, Marie conducted the company business much the same way as her old mentor Bill Donovan, cool and ruthless. After her 'disguise' at Bastogne she never changed her appearance again. Her other colleagues in the intelligence business respected and admired her. She could work nonstop on some crisis for days, then kick back and enjoy Dana, the kids and her friends. She was also the master of the compromise, the art of negotiating up to that invisible line and then not cross over. Her line was simple, Don't fuck with my family my friends or my country. The White House Chief of Staff called her several months after the election of the new president. Reagan hadn't replaced her and Marie hadn't attempted to defend her position as director. The newly elected president called her into the oval office, and after a few minutes of chit chat, asked Marie to present her credentials. She unzipped the side of her pants suit and said,

"Do you really want to see them?" Reagan was stunned. It was one of the few times in his long life that he couldn't think of a good comeback. So he leaned back in his chair and laughed, not a chuckle but a real belly buster. The DD told her that the president of the CIAB wanted an appointment. "Jesus Bob, are you the appointment secretary now?"

"Don't get on my case Marie, the call came from the

'Mans' office. "What does coal have to do with us?"

"Beats me, you're the D and I'm the D minus," he replied closing the door. When the president of one of the most powerful associations in the world stepped into Marie's office, she noted that he was polite and assured. The first thing he asked, after declining coffee, was for a private conversation. Marie nodded, pushed a button, and told him to go ahead.

"You didn't have to kill him." Marie was astonished, but like her mentor, poker was in her blood. She raised an eyebrow.

"The Senator. We were not exactly thrilled at your confirmation, but the industry has changed."

He shook his head, "I don't see how you could have done it with all of those people around."

Marie gazed at 'president' while her thoughts were racing. So Lewis must have paid Smithe a visit, and knowing Lewis he scared the shit out of him. Damn, I knew something was wrong when that fat prick almost begged the committee to approve my confirmation. So if they didn't kill him and Lewis didn't have any reason to, it must have been an accident. But… The look in her eyes changed and the quiet menace in her voice caused the man to reflexively touch his tie.

"We do not sanction US citizens. Now is there anything else I can help you with?"

She stood up and the president said, "No mam," and hurried from her office.

(*She called her secretary and told him that she wasn't to be disturbed. The Director of the Central Intelligence Agency can't be seen crying. Jeanette with her hand on my breast, little Joseph tortured by those goddamned cocksuckers, and all of those people killed for diamonds. The Hitlers' and Stalins will be in hell, but if there is any God in heaven those cynical 'business men' like Rhodes and Oppenheimer will be roasting along with them. Marie sat still looking into the past, the tears streaming down her face. She sighed and wiped her eyes. I guess the bastards get a pass this time but they'd better not cross me... ever.*)

Lewis sat in his old recliner and shucked the shells from the clip of his P-38, leaving one in the chamber. I could do this with my eye shut. He smiled, and it almost is. He lay the pistol on his lap and kicked back thinking about his life; How could one man love so many women and still be in love with each and every one. Mary, Cindy, Darnell and Mia. I would have married the first three but they were too damned smart and wouldn't have me. I love the twins and the rest of my kids, but I miss Joe and the Goat and my cat. Thank God Marie is still kicking. Speaking of God I wonder if there is one. Guess it's time to find out...

Dad was seventy-two when he developed glaucoma in his eye. He had said he would rather be dead than blind, and shot himself in the heart with his P-38. I found him the next day in his old recliner Marie came over and said that he died of natural causes and the CIA doctor concurred and signed the death certificate. He left a short note to Marie telling her to bury him in the family plot next to his tiger. The gilders were to be given to his women and kids. We were swamped with telegrams and phone calls asking that the memorial service be delayed, so his friends and families could pay their respects. There wasn't a morgue in Cottage Grove so we kept him in the cold room of his friend the butcher. Pop would have gotten a kick out of that.

The day of the funeral the small town was packed. His local friends had set up several kegs that lasted about ten minutes. It was a hot summer day and people were getting thirsty, when a Budweiser truck pulled up and started unloading. I asked Marie if it was some of her Black fund money, and she shook her head no. There were many uniforms in the crowd. Men that he had fought with in France, Korea and Vietnam, White haired veterans from Australia, and England, and even the old Montagnard Chief who was at least ninety. He had an open casket and half the crowd that passed by, laughed, as Marie had the butcher stick Pop's evil eye in the socket. Marie stood up and addressed the crowd. No eulogy or speeches, as Sergeant Major Lewis Sergeant hated speeches. Just drink up as there is a Coors truck due in ten minutes. There was no warning when a squadron of Air Force jets blasted overhead, followed by a trio from Korea, and a squadron from Australia. At twilight a bugler from the 101st blew Taps, and the funeral was over. He was buried next to his tiger who will guard his back through eternity. Marie and others mourned him but the two women that he never touched, the "Gold Dust Twins" grieved the longest. His simple headstone is inscribed:

LEWIS SERGEANT
SERGEANT MAJOR UNITED STATES ARMY

Author